Au Phuc Dup and Nowhere to Go

Fred Reed

iUniverse, Inc.
New York   Bloomington

iUniverse books may be ordered through booksellers or by contacting:

iUniverse
1663 Liberty Drive
Bloomington, IN 47403
www.iuniverse.com
1-800-Authors (1-800-288-4677)

ISBN: 978-1-4401-3720-4 (sc)
ISBN: 978-1-4401-3721-1 (ebook)

Printed in the United States of America

iUniverse rev. date: 04/1/2009

To Anesthesia Remingham who, although he doesn't exist, exactly expresses my view of Viet Nam, the military, and life in general.

EGGLESBY'S FIRST FLIGHT

Far above the glowing emerald chess board of Vietnam, Major Mike Egglesby peered from the cockpit of the F-4 with icy blue eyes the color of swimming pools, his handsome blond face twisted into a smile of death and resignation. He practiced his smile of death and resignation for several minutes each morning. The smile was going very well now, he thought, searching the ground below carefully. He was looking for some infantry to support, and they were hiding from him.

Egglesby was the worst pilot in the Air Force, but also the prettiest. His handsomeness verged on the grotesque. Tousled blonde hair rose from his sun-bronzed forehead in a golden tidal wave that almost demanded a surf board to set it off. His chin jutted forward so appealingly that his detractors, who were many, thought it looked like some sort of scoop, and the dimple that divided its forward protuberance was so deep that nature seemed to have been trying, perhaps in a fit of evolutionary whimsy, to grow a new and interesting bifurcate appendage. Above the eyes he looked like a crested cockatoo, and below, like a steam shovel.

Being the worst pilot in the Air Force did not come easy, especially when attrition in the north was forcing the Pentagon to train large numbers of replacement pilots hurriedly. The most terrible of the terrible new pilots were quickly killed, however, leaving Major Egglesby, who did not fly over the north, safe in his title.

From boyhood Major Egglesby had shown talent for being a terrible pilot. His disastrous career had begun when, as a boy of

1

eleven in the State Theater in Tuskaweegie, Michigan, he had first seen the smile of resignation and death. The movie was Forgotten Skies, a grade-H potboiler about Chenault's Flying Tigers. Tab Hunter played Rip Langley, a youthful and idealistic American crop-duster who had volunteered to keep China out of the hands of murderous squinty-eyed Japs. Late in the movie Rip had been trapped, low on fuel, above the beautiful Tsing Tsong River by twelve Zero fighters. They were led by his nemesis, Colonel Togo Fuji. Fuji was a fanatical sadist who practiced his swordsmanship by chopping up Christian children abducted from missionary homes.

Rip could have bailed out and lived to fight another day. However, he had just learned that his sweetheart back in the States had been run over by a train, leaving him with nothing to live for. The young idealist disdained to flee. Instead he stared death in the eye with a resigned and noble smile, shoved the throttle home, and dove, guns blazing, toward doom and the evil colonel. The sound of the engine rose to a scream, the guns shuddered backabaekahackabacka, and Togo Fuji's plane grew ever larger in the windscreen until ....

Young Egglesby's eyes had frosted over and he had dropped his popcorn. While mingled bits and pieces of idealistic crop duster and sadistic colonel flew through the air, Egglesby realized that he was fated to become a fighter pilot.

When puberty struck, Egglesby had burgeoned into spectacular beauty and second-string quarterback for the Tuskaweegie Bruins. He was a terrible quarterback. The coach only played him in the closing minutes of catastrophic games, when the Tuskaweegie Bruins trailed by forty points. This suited Egglesby, for whom tragedy held a strong appeal. Like military officers in general, he believed in ideals and essences instead of results, and so, smiling the Smile, he threw long, hopeless, inaccurate passes and acquiesced with manly resignation to the tragedy of life. In fact, he had once thrown a long pass while on the three-yard line of the opposing team.

He also developed Rip Langley's jocular and masculine mode of speech. "Hiya, guys," he would say in a deep bass to his pimply classmates at the Candy Shoppe soda fountain on Main Street, "Why dontcha join the Air Force with Big Daddy. Eh? Little combat and then the bars of Paris. Join the Great Game. You don't want to slave away in a bank, do you? That's not for me, my friends."

He would smile at the girls, to the venom of his less gorgeous competitors. Had anyone else said such a thing, the girls would have snickered, but no one else had a bifurcate chin.

After a pause Egglesby would say, "Sure, it's dangerous. We all know that. I might not make it back some day. Well, nobody lives forever, eh?"

In college he still dreamed of sacrifice and the warrior spirit, of the brave and the perfect and the handsome. The only book he ever read without compulsion was Beowulf. He liked to imagine himself high in the windswept hills of wintry Denmark, gazing with the smile of death and resignation at the advancing merciless hordes. Hordes of what had never concerned him. Nor, for that matter, had victory. His imaginings had never gone beyond the romance of hopeless courage, and savoring the grey adrenal satisfactions of doom.

Flight school had not treated kindly his thrusting search for virility and extinction. The instructors quickly noticed that he couldn't fly. Sometimes they suspected he wasn't especially interested in flying. His emphasis was on mood over technique, his preference for the brave and spectacular in place of the practical. Once on a night flight, while concentrating on the poetic essence of combat, he had failed to concentrate on his altimeter and nearly rammed a water tower.

He had barely graduated because of academic insufficiency. What, he had wondered as he sat in his room struggling with definite integrals, occasionally stopping to smile into the shaving mirror over the desk—what had slide rules and hyperbolic functions to do with the hot flowing essences of a warrior's soul? Fortunately the demand for pilots was urgent, and his eagerness was judged to compensate for a certain lack of acuity.

Arriving at Danang well after his reputation, Major Egglesby reported to the wing commander, Colonel Dravidian, for assignment.

"Major Michael Egglesby reporting for duty, sir," he said, clicking his heels to attention and pointing his chin at Dravidian.

"At ease, Egglesby. And don't make so much noise. This isn't the Luftwaffe."

Dravidian was a dark and shapeless man with a hairless cue ball of a head and a sour outlook on life. He looked at Egglesby with a vague sense that something was wrong. What was it, he wondered? Ah, that was it: The major looked as though he had been hit in the chin with an ax.

"You're going to be with the 443rd Tac Fighter squadron, close air support in the area. The squadron commander will tell you everything you need to know. Now get out of here."

Major Egglesby was distraught. This wasn't what lie had joined the Air Force for.

"But...the action's up north! Can't I...I mean...." Somehow Colonel Dravidian didn't look like a man who would understand ideals and essences.

"Somebody's got to stir up mud for the grunts, Major. You're it. Don't give me a lot of guff. I hear enough of it as it is."

Month after month Dravidian watched green pilots come into his office, eager to bomb worthless targets in the north. Month after month he wrote their mothers to explain why they were dead. This was difficult, because he didn't know why they were dead.

"Goddammit, sir! It isn't fair. Let me carry the ball! I want to make the big play up north, sir. Give me a chance!"

He smiled his boyish smile of eagerness. He knew how to appeal to authority because he had seen Rock Hudson do it, in a movie about a star quarterback making a comeback from an iron lung.

Colonel Dravidian hadn't seen the movie.

"Nuts, Egglesby. Anyway, you couldn't hit Hanoi. It isn't big enough."

Judging by his flight school transcript, thought Colonel Dravidian, it might be safer to assign the major to Thailand. Major Egglesby did not seem the sort of man you wanted overhead with bombs.

The next day Major Egglesby had climbed into his F-4 on his first combat flight. "The old bird ready, sergeant?" he said to the crew chief. "Greased and oiled? Ha-ha." It paid to josh with the enlisted men, he thought. It showed largeness of soul.

He was in a hopeful mood. He would prove himself in the south and be sent north later as a reward. Maybe it would not be so humiliating to brave a mere hail of ground fire in the south. He might even find a worthy opponent.

"Yes sir, she's ready," said the crew chief, figuring that the Air Force must be running out of pilots.

Major Egglesby pushed his cataract of hair into his helmet, cranked the engines, shoved the throttles forward, and began his roll. The engines howled like the voice of fate, like mournful dragons going to their deaths against hopeless odds. The green ugly airplane sailed into the air. Then, peering down from eight thousand feet over the checkered green world below he waited until the call came from Marines in need. Ten minutes later he heard through static.

"Bravo One Five to bird on station."

Major Egglesby responded immediately with enthusiasm.

"Roger. Tell me where to put them. Ha-ha. Tell old Charlie I'm going to drop my wad right in the old hip pocket, smack on his helmet. He's going to be nothing but hair, teeth, and eyeballs," he said, dredging up phrases from old movies. He wasn't supposed to talk that way on the radio, hut he knew that combat minimized formality.

"Uh, yeah. We got a sniper in the tree line. I've got two men down," came the urgent voice from below. Can you lay'em 100 yards north of that funny-looking temple? I'll mark with smoke."

"Rodger. You got it, fella."

Purple smoke puffed against the green near the tree line. His heart thumping, Major Egglesby pushed the stick over and dove, his face alight with the joy of battle. The F-4 screamed down toward glowing viridian squares that grew rapidly before the shuddering plane. A taut grin came over his face. Sunlight gleamed from his gauges, glinted from Plexiglas. The sneering face of Colonel Togo Fuji rose in his mind, and the Christian children chopped into bits. He pickled off the bombs and pulled from the dive into a streaking run-out over the paddies.

"Well, guys, did the Big Boy get'em?" he asked exultantly, watching the paddies streak by at 500 feet and feeling a sense of calm and purity. He was made for combat, he thought.

A long silence was broken by a roar of static "You crazy

sonofabitch! North of the fucken smoke. Your other left! You just wrecked my motherfucken truck."

By the end of his first week, Major Egglesby had bombed an amtrac platoon by mistake, almost killed a company of surrounded Marines with a misplaced napalm drop, and provided close-air support for a trash-burning detail from base whose smoke he mistook for a marker. The infantry, scared to death, stopped calling for support when Major Egglesby was on station. He just flew in big circles until he ran low on fuel and had to dump off his bombs in the ocean, and then land. It was a crushing blow to his ideals and essences.

For a while he tried to get targets by changing his voice and lying about his call sign, but he fooled no one. Someone, he suspected, was tipping off the grunts. For practical purposes, he was out of the war. Sometimes he bombed a tree line just to have something to do, but it wasn't the same. He became despondent. Soon he took to sitting alone in has hooch with a bottle of Jack Daniels.

INTELLIGENCE AT ITS BEST

Major Rudyard Thackeray Toute, in charge of Division Intelligence, closed the door to his office and climbed onto his desk chair, where he stood holding three paper airplanes. He was preparing the daily intelligence estimate for I Corps. The first airplane was labeled in Major Toute's small, precise handwriting, "Probable Attack." The second said "Suspected Enemy Concentration." The third said "Infiltration Route."

He stood teetering on one leg, which made it more challenging to aim, and threw the first airplane at Danang on the map of I Corps that covered an entire wall. It made a slight "click" as it struck. Major Toute went to look where it had hit, and wrote "Au Phuc Dup Hamlet, Probable Attack" on a pad. Then he went back to his chair to determine suspected enemy concentrations. He did this daily, alerting the American forces to the intentions of the Viet Cong.

The slight click came from the paper clip that Colonel Toute attached to the nose of his airplanes to tighten his groups. He had started using the paper clips several months before, and he had so increased his accuracy that Infiltration Routes and Suspected Enemy Concentrations had moved much closer to Danang than they had been. The Pentagon had noticed that the communists were tightening their grip on the city, and had requested two more divisions.

Major Toute didn't have a clue what was actually happening in Vietnam. Nor did anyone else in the Intelligence Office.

This had bothered him at first, but then he had learned that the lack of information did not hinder him in the performance of his duty. Now he was quite comfortable with things. In fact, any intrusion of the VC into his affairs would have seemed an imposition.

Besides, he had no choice. No American on his staff, or anywhere else for that matter, spoke Vietnamese. A year earlier the Marine Corps had begun sending students to language school at Henderson Hall in Washington, but they had never showed the slightest capacity to learn Vietnamese in Washington. Since the supply of Viet-speaking Marines remained inadequate, after six months the brass had doubled the number of students sent to learn Vietnamese. They didn't, and so the quota was again doubled. No matter how many Marines didn't learn Vietnamese, the need remained the same and the school expanded. Its budget, grew like a weed to accommodate the burgeoning number of unlearning students, and the commander was promoted. Meanwhile the intelligence people had to rely on hired translators, all of whom were Viet Cong officers in disguise.

To make matters worse, General Grommett didn't like the intelligence departments. He had once said with what he hoped was Patton-like soldierly bluntness, "The gooks are the enemy. You don't study enemies. You kill them." At least Colonel Walther, who had written this oration for him, said it sounded Pattonesque.

General Grommett resented the intelligence people for much the same reasons why he resented the Viet Cong, viewing them both as impediments to the smooth prosecution of the war. They added a disagreeable uncertainty to things, and caused embarrassing diversions of the war effort from its proper concern of maximizing the tonnage of bombs dropped. Without the Viet Cong it would be easier to bomb and strafe and keep his numbers up. General Grommett didn't see why he had to have an intelligence department. He didn't know much about the Viet Cong, and believed it un-American to find out. He thought it unsoldierly to study an enemy he didn't respect, and how could one respect little yellow peckerheads who hid under trees so you couldn't. bomb them?

The intelligence office, unable to find out what was going on, had used Yankee ingenuity in discovering ways of doing its job, which, Major Toute had been gratified to find, was not to know what was happening but to turn out intelligence reports. His staff had found many ways of doing this. For months, every Wednesday they had predicted a major attack, qualifying the prediction by saying that tactical conditions to the south might force the enemy to change his plans. On Thursday through Tuesday, they predicted quiet, adding that tactical conditions to the north might force the enemy to strike.

To keep up the volume of reports, which they had noticed seemed to govern promotions, they had simply reissued reports from the same period the year before. Since no one stayed in Vietnam for more than a year, the recycling was never noticed, and last year's predictions were no less accurate than this year's. The staff had learned to phrase estimates with a Delphic opacity that fitted all possible events, like a horoscope.

A tremendous flow of estimates, situation reports, prognostications, and statistics issued from the department. The office was going swimmingly well even before the paper-airplane method of collecting intelligence had been developed.

Major Toute put on his hat and opened the door, which was marked Head, REBOP, which meant Reinforcement Evaluation Board/Operations. He was going downtown to talk to the chief bellhop at the hotel where he did his drinking. The bellhop was his chief source of tactical information. Next week he had to produce a report on the Political Situation, Trends, and Mood of the Populace.

Egglesby Confronts Destiny

Major Egglesby finally broke. Jack Daniels was insufficient solace. He could no longer bear to fly endlessly in circles above the rice while every infantry outfit for miles around hid from him. For a while he had managed to find an occasional rifle company that hadn't heard of him. Once a company had been supported by Egglesby, however, it went into hiding. Now the infantry maintained radio silence so that he couldn't even be sure they were down there.

For weeks he tried every trick he could think of. Sometimes he got on the radio in what he hoped was a Mexican accent.

"Thees ees Bravo-4-9 weeth a fool load of 20 mike-mike. Eenybody needs help?"

Silence. The ground-pounders knew his F-4 had taken off.

"Eet ees a sad day, amigos. The major that fly thees plane before, he ees dead. A tank, eet run over heem, so now I am flying for heem."

Nothing.

"Aw, come on."

Someone below keyed a radio below and a loud raspberry erupted in major Egglesby's earphones. There was no other reply. Even the Viet Cong were frightened of Major Egglesby. They knew the tactics of the other pilots and could usually tell where the bombs would fall. They simply made sure they were somewhere else. With Major Egglesby, nothing worked but prayer.

Major Egglesby had appealed to everybody who had the authority to help, but without results. Colonel Dravidian, longing for his trout streams and no longer seeing any particular point to the war, didn't want to send Major Egglesby up north to die bombing a toolshed. Nor did he want the infantry to be killed by Major Egglesby's essentially random bombing. General Drinelly wasn't interested as long as Egglesby flew and kept Drinelly's sortie rate up. The ordinance depot didn't care as long as Egglesby took the correct number of bombs and didn't bring them back. The maintenance people were happy because the F-4 never got shot up, so they didn't have to repair it. The system was working smoothly as things were, and no one wanted Major Egglesby to bollix the works by demanding to bomb things. Besides, the infantry insisted passionately that there were no targets.

Finally Major Egglesby hit on the answer. One afternoon he took off and immediately dumped his bombs at sea. He had gotten in the habit of doing this early because it made the plane more pleasant to fly. Then he came back over land and climbed to 30,000 feet a few miles west of Monkey Mountain.

Major Egglesby turned off the radio entirely. It was against regulations, but he was beyond caring about regulations. Major Egglesby was a desperate man.

Then he armed the cannon and checked his gauges. Next he carefully scanned the sky.

To the north, ominous specks came over the horizon.

"One-five Bravo, this is Three-seven Alpha. MiGs!" he called into the microphone in controlled but urgent tones. "Bandits at heading 334, closing fast! They mean business. Am engaging! Am engaging!"

He yanked the stick and turned hard toward the lead nonexistent MiG, shoving the throttle to full afterburner. The Phantom lurched forward and began to pick up speed. The MiG responded by diving earthward and evading to the right. The other MiGs stayed on course: So, thought Major Egglesby, it was single combat? He was willing to play that game. He reversed his turn, pulling 5 G's, and panted explosively to relieve the terrible weight on his chest.

Dropping like an eagle onto the tail of the leader, Major Egglesby felt his thumb closing on the trigger as a resolute smile played across his lips, tinged by doom. He snapped off a long burst of 20 mike-mike, the skies shuddering with its heavy thump. Missed! The MiG was a worthy opponent. He cut hard and fired again, closer this time....

For half an hour the one-plane dogfight raged in the puzzled skies of Asia. Soon not a single non-existent MiG remained. Then, gun empty, Major Egglesby banked toward base. He felt strangely happy. Maybe it wasn't the real thing, he thought, but it wasn't bad. In this war, he was beginning to realize, you took what you could get.

THE STRAFING OF GROMMETT

When godless atheists attacked the Field Grade compound, an assault that brought on Operation Ballpeen Duck and saved Danang temporarily for democracy, General Grommett was swimming in the pool by the bar. He swam daily to keep fit. The keys to becoming Chairman of the JCS were not making enemies, caring for the common soldier, and Looking Every Inch a General. No one with a pot belly had ever become chief of staff. On the other hand, many whose only qualification was a flat stomach had.

However, other problems presented themselves. Third Tracs had been hit several times recently by the VC. There was this nonsense about invisible airplanes. He would have to think about these things.

Just before the onslaught began, General Grommett poised himself for a dramatic moment on the end of the diving board, maneuvered his toes over the edge for a better grip, and looked around with an air of command. He assumed his air of command by poking his chest out, slightly elevating his chin, and frowning.

"Alley oop," he said to himself, sprang lightly into the air and cut the water with a clean scloop.

Several colonels idly watched him and sipped drinks brought by scurrying Vietnamese waitresses in PX uniforms. They always watched him because of the curious expression he assumed before diving. Some thought he might be having a minor stroke, but others insisted it was impossible to have so many minor strokes in a row, and that the general must have some sort of neck trouble. Another school held that he had an intermittent form of Parkinson's disease, but they were held to be extremists. He swam to the end of the pool with graceful strokes that displayed his athletic nature and....

Suddenly a sharp crack-crack-crack shattered his reverie. A row of bright orange flashes appeared magically across the compound, tearing deep holes in the concrete. Shrapnel whizzed viciously through the air. Colonels dived for the deck and waitresses screamed. General Grommett hugged the earth and low-crawled toward a row of sandbags for partial protection. Jesus, he thought, it's true. We've been strafed—but there were no aircraft.

High over Monkey Mountain an airplane spun out of control and plummeted toward the earth, its cockpit shattered by a well-aimed burst of twenty mike-mike. The dying pilot clutched the stick with weakening hands, realizing in his final moments that he had met his match in a simple American crop-duster. It was Colonel Togo Fuji....

Half an hour later, the strafing apparently over, General Grommett retired to a chaise longue with what he hoped was a fine display of insouciance under fire. "Waxer!" he bellowed.

Colonel Waxer jumped up and hurried over. "Yessir?"

General Grommett signed to his favorite waitress for his customary drink, gin and tonic with double lemon, and said to Colonel Waxer, "Danang is in danger."

"Yessir?" said Colonel Waxer, wondering what the general meant. There hadn't been much action near Danang for some time, except the recurrent attacks on the amtrac compound. No matter how much Colonel Waxer strengthened the forces around Third Tracs, the VC always got through. It disturbed him.

"Colonel," General Grommett whispered, leaning forward, "The communists are gathering their strength to deliver us a Big Blow. They are getting ready to capture Danang. If they succeed, it will be a Kick in the Balls for the war. All the forces of treason and godless atheism in Congress will demand that we pull out of Vietnam. We'll have to lower our quotas of artillery shells. We'll be driven out of Asia, step by step, as the communist hordes sweep across Southeast Asia like a cancerous malignancy."

"Yessir?"

General Grommett's voice dropped another couple of decibels. "Have you looked at the map?"

"Yessir." Actually Colonel Waxer hadn't. For the first few months of his tour he had tried, but nothing on the map seemed to have any relation to what was actually out there on the ground. Finally he had given up on maps.

General Grommett said, "You have been here less time than I have. When you spend enough time in war, you develop a sense for it, an intuition."

"Yessir."

"The Vietcong battalions are drawing closer to the city. Constantly they tighten the ring—but they don't attack. They're keeping inconspicuous. Why?"

"Yessir."

"Except for the amtrac compound. They have now hit the tracs eleven times in five weeks. Charlie is making a determined effort, for devious reasons only the communist mentality can fathom, to eliminate that one compound. Why?"

"Yessir."

"What makes the tracs so important to them?"

"Yessir."

"Then come the invisible airplanes. Who knows what fiendish technology Ivan has given Charlie? Why are the invisible airplanes only at Danang?"

He pondered the inscrutable communist mind for a moment.

"They're concentrating. Quietly, to lull us into a false sense of security. We've got to hit them first, break up their forces. I want you to draw up plans for a big op, search and destroy, to Au Phuc Dup Hamlet. We've got to clean them out, stop the infection from spreading."

General Grommett waited for Colonel Waxer to say "Yessir," which seemed to be the only thing he knew how to say.

"Yessir."

"Goddamit, can you say anything except Yessir?"

"Yessir.... "

"Well, do it."

"Yessir."

General Grommett frowned. Colonel Waxer was hard to talk to. It was like talking to himself. He sipped his gin-and-tonic and thought about the operation to Au Phuc Dup. Here was a chance to shine. It would be a division-strength operation, he decided, with tanks and amtracs and every available helicopter, heavy artillery preparation, and maybe even naval gunfire. No, that was a bad idea. The Navy would try to steal his show. The prospects for his image were very good, he decided. With a little luck, operation Ballpeen Duck would be the biggest military operation since the Inchon Landing. It would route the massive forces the communists were obviously collecting, and save Danang. And he would command it.

WE MEET FEINSTEIN

Ezekiel Feinstein, newest member of AP's Danang bureau, stared at the keyboard of a portable typewriter in the deserted press hooch. It was five a.m. Outside in the steaming darkness of Asia, artillery boomed as batteries fired randomly to keep their quotas up. Feinstein didn't notice. He was worrying about what it meant to be Jewish. He was also sweating profusely although he was stripped to his skivvy shorts. Sweat ran down his long thin legs, matting the black hairs in sodden streaks. Feinstein was probably the hairiest man in Viet Nam. He had thick hair on his wrists, fur on his legs, a lush mat on his chest, and a dark halo of fine down on his earlobes. Even his friends said he looked like a yak-hair pillow on stilts, or several pounds of stalked lint.

He was depressed because he had been in Vietnam for six weeks and had not gotten a big story. When he was depressed he always worried and felt vaguely guilty—not guilty of anything, but just guilty. Often he worried about being Jewish. What it was that worried him about being Jewish wasn't clear to him, which worried him more. At the moment he wondered whether he hadn't betrayed his people by changing his name. His father had always been contemptuous of Jews who changed their names.

Feinstein had been born Hezekiah Baum in Hoboken, son of a struggling fancy-foods jobber in the lush half-Spanish neighborhoods near the railroad. He grew up happily enough, playing street ball with tired baseballs with flaps hanging down like a spaniel's ears, feeling up the girls behind the weeds in vacant lots, and reading. Everybody had problems, so he didn't know he had a problem. His parents were good to him. They were, however, working like dogs to save tuition for him, and his father made it clear that either he made A's or he found another family. He made A's.

In the pacifistic mood prevailing in the early Sixties at Oklahoma University School of Journalism, where he went because he got a scholarship, he had discovered that being Jewish was a burden. At least, being a pacifist named H. Baum was a burden, and he wouldn't have been named Baum if he had been Irish. Being hairy hadn't helped. His friends had started calling him H-Bomb the Hoboken Tarantula. At parties a predictable exchange always took place.

"DeWayne, this is H. Baum. He's in journalism."

"Aitch Bomb? That's his name? You shittin' me."

"I swear. Don't piss him off. He's got a short fuse."

His self-esteem collapsed. He began walking parallel to sidewalks at a distance of fifteen feet to avoid being introduced to anyone. He grew moody, took to sitting in remote corners of the library and reading tales of suicide and decay. His grades suffered. The thought of going through life as H-Bomb the Hoboken Tarantula loomed before him. Finally he snapped. He went to the courthouse and changed his name to Feinstein. Ever since, he had worried about having changed his name. He had never told his father, who would have been ashamed at having a name-changing Jew for a son.

His father, puzzled at getting dozens of telephone calls for Ezekiel Feinstein, had been complaining to the phone company ever since.

Feinstein was also worried about not having a big story. He disapproved of the war, but he wanted a Pulitzer. Vietnam was his big chance, everybody's big chance. If a reporter couldn't find a story here, he would never find one. A raging sense of urgency weighed on him, a fear that the war was on the brink of some miraculous finish that would leave him high and dry, Pulitzerless. Every time anything big happened, Feinstein was always somewhere else. Maybe he was doomed.

The flap opened and the driver assigned him for the day walked in, that guy Hearn he saw around. Some hind of chemistry major. Feinstein hated chemistry.

"Morning, sir. Monkey Mountain...."

"Yeah. Yeah, forgot. Let's go, I guess." Feinstein grabbed a canteen belt and camera bag. Radar sites on Monkey Mountain. Big deal. They were there to guard against air attack, but the enemy didn't have airplanes. Meanwhile the artillery shot at enemies who weren't there, and progress was measured by counting corpses that hadn't been killed. Feinstein wondered what the Viet Cong contributed to the war. Apparently it could be fought perfectly adequately without them. Increasingly he suspected that it was being fought without them.

Outside the gate Hearn inched the jeep delicately through the mass of Viet children trying to sell their sisters, peddle dirty pictures, or map the base for mortar attacks.

"Hey Joe. Joe. Hey Joe," ooched a boy of perhaps eight years. "You want boomboom? Boocoo cheap. My sister. Clean. Long time. Sucky fucky."

Hearn answered, "Sister no good. How about your mother. She virgy?"

"Yeah, Joe, boocoo. You want? I go get."

"If she virgy, where you come from?"

"My sister have me. No problem. 1 get?"

"Oh, fuck off."

The throng thinned and they headed down the red clay roadcut toward the mountain.

"Well, Hearn, what's the hot scoop? You get around a lot. I need a Pulitzer this morning."

"Yessir...."

"Stop calling me sir. It makes me nervous."

"Yeah. Sorry." Feinstein wasn't much older than Hearn, really. "It's a habit. If you call people sir, they don't talk to you. Stories ... I don't know. Not much. I did meet some guys out at Marble Mountain, say they got strafed yesterday."

"Strafed? Air Force hit the good guys again?"

That might be a story. Too common, though.

"No, he says nobody did it. I mean, rounds came out of nowhere. I didn't pay much attention. You hear a lot of shit like that. Like flying saucers in those grocery store magazines."

"How can rounds come out of nowhere?"

"Well, maybe that's where they were, so they had to

Hearn wasn't always easy to talk to. It sounded anything was better than looking at a bunch of' rad quonset huts.

"Can you take me to Marble Mountain?"

"Can you get me a fifth of Jim Beam?"

"Deal."

WE ENCOUNTER
AX PERDIEM, WONDERINGLY

iple canopy of IV Corps near the Lao border, a lethal
nen tended to disappear without a trace, or would have
stream splashed and chuckled through the cathedral
mmense vegetation. Thick vines the color of bamboo
from the trees in great sworls. On the broad surfaces
hes like fat green sausages waited in the brooding
drop down any passing collar. This was Special Forces
territory.

Thirty feet above the dancing water, the foliage was parted
furtively. A pair of piercing brown eyes peered into the gloom. The
eyes rested deep in hollow sockets in an emaciated face, emaciated by
hunger not physical but of the soul. The forehead rose like sunburned
leather to a shaven head. A thin white scar snaked down his face like
frozen lightning.

The scar belonged to Major Maxwell Perdion, universally known
to his compadres in Third Special Forces Group as Max Perdiem. He
had gotten the scar by slipping on a plate of barbecue left by a drunk
on the floor of the Officer's Club at Won San, Korea, and falling into
a floor lamp. It made him look like an alert but puzzled skull en route
to a Halloween party, an appearance much esteemed in the Special
Forces. At the moment he was crouching in the crotch of a tree,
preparing to cross the stream on a bridge of vines. Perdiem was on a
secret mission.

21

Squatting low on the vines, he emerged as silently as the shadow of death into the sunlight. He held a Stoner carbine, loaded and ready, the coppery points of bullets glinting dully in the magazine. As he started across the gulf he motioned stealthily. From the green dimness three Montagnards sitting on a branch of the tree prepared to follow.

Just as Perdiem reached the midpoint of the bridge, a badly tied knot parted and the bridge sagged sharply.

"Ooo-oo-aaaaaaaaaaaagh!," hollered Perdiem, flailing wildly. The bridge collapsed further.

"Waa-aaagh!" shouted Perdiem, waving one leg for balance. The carbine dropped.

Oh, hell, Perdiem thought, it was happening again. He wasn't paranoid. All evidence accumulated over a long career indicated that the world really was out to get him. By now he expected it.

For a moment that seemed endless he stood on the toe of one foot, arms outspread in a desperate quest for balance. He looked like Apollo poised for flight, or a ballerina attempting a new and demanding movement without enough coffee. Then he teetered frantically and toppled in the manner of a collapsing obelisk with a long quavering shriek.

"Aaaa-a-aaaaaahhhh—-agghhhhhhhhhh-eeeee-waggg!"

He hit the water with a gargantuan splash. A moment later he surfaced, coughing and spitting water. "Goddamit it all!" he shouted and kicked a tree stump, "It worked in the fucking manual!" The Montagnards watched patiently. They knew him well.

At the Special Forces base nearby, several men sat around the campfire fiddling through cardboard for the edible parts of C-rations. A lieutenant with the lantern-shaped features that come out of the hollers of Kentucky drawled, "Sounds like Boo Boo did it again."

"Yeah. Poor dumb sonofabitch."

"Goddam Army oughta issue him a mother."

Boo Boo Perdiem was a legend in a service replete with legends. His ineptitude for war was boundless. So far as living memory could recall, Max had never done anything right. No one was sure why. He was physically fit. He was brave. A pschiatrist had attested that he fell withing the admittedly broad mental limits considered normal in Special Forces. He was eager. He had all the credentials, including the scar. The Special Forces didn't worry about the source of a scar, as long as it was prominent.

Still, it was well known that Boo Boo couldn't get a drink of water without breaking his leg, losing his rifle, and setting off NORAD alarms. He invariably went north when he was supposed to go south. If he parachuted, he got caught in a tree and hung there like a Christmans ornament until rescued. On night scuba missions, he got his compass bearing wrong and bubbled off into mid-Pacific. No one understood why. Nor did anyone care.

As long as he looked like a skull, he was welcome in the Special Forces. Perdiem had shown a flair for special warfare from early in life. In his small Oklahoma town of Tusker, where his father had been half of the police force, Max had begun collecting knives—hunting knives, fighting knives, kitchen knives, strange triangular combat knives from Java that were advertised in the backs of men's magazines. He hung them on the walls of his room, fondled them, and occasionally sat on them and got cut. Max was not then sure why he liked knives, but when he went hunting during his adolescence, he always carried several with him.

Somehow Max hadn't quite fitted with the other boys of the town. He had declined to play baseball in the weedy overgrown lot at the edge of town, preferring instead to stalk the third-baseman in the high grass in left field. He gave up the practice after Johnny Huston had gone back for a pop foul and stepped on his hand, breaking three fingers.

When compelled by the school authorities to join the team, he had devised an exploding baseball. It blew up in his back pocket on the school bus, necessitating an undignified trip to the doctor and a curious bandage. He had almost been thrown out of college when the night maid had opened a linen closet and found him standing inside like a fierce and scrawny owl, apparently practicing lurking. Actually he had read that remaining still and silent for hours was a major difficulty for elite reconnaissance units, which by now he had decided he wanted to enter.

Which proved easy.

At Fort Polk he had been immediately recognized as Special

Forces material, meaning that he could hike with staggering loads for unreasonable distances, but did so many things wrong that the company commander was willing to do anything to have him go somewhere else. This was not unusual, as the real Army generally regarded the Forces as an internal asylum.

Perdiem had promptly had shinnied up a parachute tower to do chin-ups at 100 feet, an act conveying high caste, but had gotten stuck and

couldn't get down. The base hook-and-ladder team had saved him. In Special Forces training at Fort Bragg, he had hidden in a Dempster Dumpster during infiltration training, unfortunately just as the garbage truck arrived, with the result that he was very nearly compacted. But he jumped out of airplanes with abandon and looked death in the eye without flinching, like one skull peering at another. He said things like, "It's a good morning to die. Let's go jump."

And so he prospered, leaving behind him a trail of disaster.

His talent for catastrophe was why he had been assigned to this particular unit in the thin salient of jungle, known as the Annamese Finger, that ran from the highlands almost to Au Phuc Dup Hamlet. There were no VC for miles in any direction, for the straightforward reason that there was nothing in this remote junlge to.interest the VC, or anyone else. There wasn't much to interest the Special Forces, either. They were there because they were trained to fight in jungle, and there was no other jungle nearby. The Army had wanted them to come down to the lowlands where the VC were, but the commanding general of Special Forces had said that it never paid to let the enemy dictate your choice of ground.

The absence of VC meant that they controlled their area, suffered no losses as long as they stayed out of their own mine fields, and were never attacked. Since very few outfits controlled their areas, the command in Danang was delighted and wouldn't think of moving them. They had recently received a Unit Commendation Medal. In fact, not having men in the Annamese Finger was perhaps the greatest tactical mistake the VC had made. They could have guaranteed that no unit whatever controlled its area.

MacNamara himself, the Secretary of Defense, had noticed them on the computer printouts and pointed to them as evidence that well-trained troops could pacify Vietnam. He had showed up at a press briefing in the Pentagon several times, waving long swaths of computer printout. As usual he looked like a successful banker from a medium-sized city. His small steel-rimmed eyes gleamed from his small, steel-rimmed mind. The result was to provide the only place in Asia where Max Perdiem was unlikely to hurt himself.

And now he was in the jungle with his Montagnards on a secret mission. He was puzzled himself. Earlier that week, a helicopter had flown in, staying high to avoid ground fire from the VC who weren't there. Since the VC hadn't attacked, it was assumed that staying at altitude was tactically effective. The chopper had landed in the small clearing that served as air field, and a dozen rangy men had watched as a rear-echelon mother-fucker had gotten off, a sad pogue without a scar to his name. Colonel Billy Joel Walther had flown in as a special emissary from General Grommett. Colonel Walther's instructions were to have the Special Forces comb the jungle for the runways used by the invisible airplanes.

A jungle didn't seem a likely place for a runway, but everywhere else had been dropped by a process of elimination. Besides, who knew what a runway for invisible airplanes might look like? It might itself be invisible. In fact, you might not know when you had found it.

Major Perdiem had walked into the headquarters hooch with the poised grace of a great cat. His eyes glittered deep in their sockets. Colonel Walther had watched with unease. There was something of the outlaw about him, common with the Special Forces.

"Yessir?"

"Major, I am here to assign you a mission from General Grommett himself," said Walther importantly.

"What is it, sir?"

"I can't ell you."

"Uh…how's that again, sir?"

"I know it sounds strange, Major. There is… there are things going on that are classified. At the…." He paused significantly. "Highest level. The very highest. General Grommett has reason to believe that certain…things relating other things may be found in this sector. Your job is to go out and find them."

Perdiem stared. He was used to the Army, but this was excessive even for the Army.

"Can't you give me a hint?"

"Well…."

"Come on, just a little one."

Colonel Walther looked at him solemnly, then said, "Ooooooo oooo*ooooooooooooooooooooooooooooooooooooooo*," in a rising tone, like a jet coming in on a strafing run.

"Ah," said Perdiem after a moment.

"Yes. You are to report immediately upon finding…what you are looking for."

And so Perdiem had gathered the things he needed: a week's rations, coded radio, jungle hammock, blowgun and three boxes of poisoned darts, a compass disguised as a button, infrared night scope, a garrote, and a small Special Forces hymnal containing the worlds to all of Barry Sadler's songs. With his three Montagnards, he had set out into the trackless wastes under the impression that he was looking for trains. Colonel Walther had made a sound just like a train whistle. Perhaps the North Vietnamese were trying to improve their logistics with a rail line.

Later that afternoon at the Special Forces camp there was heard a faint, "Yeeeeeee-aaaaaaaaahh!" followed by the crump of a grenade.

One of the men relaxing at the base camp said, "Musta found that big ravine."

"Wonder why the grenade?"

"Probably figured he was ambushed."

"Poor Boo Boo."

AN ENGINEERING SOLUTION

The Air Force 707 approached Danang at high altitude to avoid the cloud of F-4s taking off to drop napalm on railroad tracks. Then it corkscrewed down to the airfield to avoid ground fire. Life in Viet Nam, as even the airplanes seemed to know, consisted chiefly of avoiding one thing or another. As the plane taxied up to the passenger terminal, a jeep raced toward it with an American flag fluttering on the bumper. Colonel Billy Joel Walther, press secretary to General Grommett, leaped out and waited while sweating marines put the ramp in place.

"Don't forget proper military courtesy," Walther fussed at his driver. "The Marine Corps will be judged by our actions."

"Yessir," said Corporal Hearn, waiting with helmet, flak jacket, and burgeoning pride. The engineers on the 707 were coming to investigate his very own invisible airplanes, in which he had come to take paternal pleasure. Almost daily he described their endlessly varied exploits to Feinstein, who put them in the paper, which disturbed General Grommett, who alarmed the Pentagon, which was now sending engineers to see Hearn's airplanes, which by their nature could not be seen. Now Hearn got to see the engineers. He was immensely satisfied with his hobby. He regarded himself as an important part of the war effort.

"Wait here," snapped Walther with what he hoped was just the right mixture of authority and cordiality for dealing with enlisted men. He had learned in OCS to regard soldiers as wily but essentially helpless. They could dig holes if told where, and could do mysterious blue-collar things to trucks, but could not be trusted to change their socks. That was what officers were for, he had concluded, to make sure the men changed their socks.

"Yessir," said Hearn, wishing that Walther would cut the crap. He suspected that Walther really wanted him to say, "Yes, Bwana." Hearn had come to the conclusion that officers were essentially helpless, especially this one. Mostly they just told you to change socks when you didn't need to, but they couldn't fix trucks.

The forward door of the 707 opened like an aluminum sepulcher. Two radar engineers from General Dynamics stepped blinking into the sunlight, wearing blue jeans and fruit boots. Colonel Walther frowned with sudden disapproval. They looked like hippies or dangerous dissidents, or maybe even godless atheists. Perhaps there was some mistake.

Mark Lehrner was a tall rangy engineer with the luxuriant red-brown mustache of a Mexican bandido and a great hawkish ski-slope of a nose. He peered around him with the sardonic curiosity of a sane man forced to visit an asylum. In fact, this was precisely how he regarded himself. His companion, Dick Potter, was rounded and pink with his hair receding from a forehead that looked like an incompletely evolved beachball. There was something haphazard and undisciplined about the pair, something profoundly unmilitary. Colonel Walther decided to request that they not set a Bad Example for the men.

"This is it, John Wayne. Keep your head down. Don't fire until you see the whites of their eyes," Lehrner said in a staccatto Jersey accent. He pulled his head down low under a floppy duck-hunting hat. Lehrner was fundamentally unimpressed by everything except good engineering. He surveyed the sprawling haze-enshrouded expanse of Vietnam, all bright greens fading to misty blues in the distance.

Potter looked calmly around. He too suspected that he had arrived in a vast peninsular looney bin, but he also suspected it would be amusing. The officious man waving his arms by the jeep had potential, he decided.

"It looks as if that guy with the cretinous grin is waiting for us," said Potter. "At least, I'm afraid he is."

"Yep."

"Answer me, Lehrner. Are we really here to look for invisible airplanes?"

"No shit, Kemo Sabe."

They clattered down the steps. "Hello, gentlemen!" said Walther with a firm military handshake. This consisted in slapping the other's hand as if swatting a ping-pong ball and squeezing firmly, like a machine tool. He had seen it done by the Rangers.

"Welcome to Danang, Republic of Viet Nam. We can take groundfire so do put on the flak jackets in the jeep. The ride to Monkey Mountain takes about half an hour. As you know, General Grommett regards your mission with highest priority. He is very worried that these mysterious airplanes may be threatening the common soldier. As you may have read in the media, the General is deeply concerned with the welfare of the common soldier. The general would like to see you afterwards and...."

"Goddam pretty scenery," said Lehrner as they scrambled into the jeep. He found it hard to focus on what Walther was saying, if anything. The metal of the jeep was so hot it was painful to touch. He was looking at Marble Mountain rising in the distance like a square green thumb.

"...of course, we'll provide you with all assistance needed to accomplish your mission and...."

It was not hard to ignore Walther. In fact, it was hard not to ignore Walther..

"That lumpish grey object would seem to be a water buffalo," said Potter. "I didn't think they really existed. What's a buffalo doing on an air base? Do you suppose we're training them to fly?"

Lehrner said, "That one is eating and defecating. Simultaneously."

Colonel Walther stopped talking for a moment. Eating and....? He began to suspect that Lehrner wasn't On The Team. He would have to warn General Grommett.

"Shall I head for Monkey Mountain, sir?" asked Hearn. He liked the newcomers. Only ten minutes in country, and they understood the war.

"Yes, and drive carefully," Colonel Walther replied.

They bounced through countryside peppered with thatched villages, past grey stolid buffalo wondering what it would be like to gore a Caucasian, past wizened mama-sans thinking their unimaginable wizened thoughts, past swarming yellow children yelling "Gimme chop-chop." Lehrner watched the alien landscape with interest, beginning to sweat beneath the luxurious overhang of his moustache. He wondered what the United States thought it was doing here. He also wondered what he himself was doing here. Lehrner had a low tolerance for fools. He had a strong premonition that he had encountered one in Colonel Walther. Something was wrong, he thought. But what? This invisible airplane business was embarrassing. The United States was far ahead of the Soviets in radar, and if Lehrner had no idea how to make an invisible airplane, neither did Ivan.

Besides, there was something weirdly unserious about the whole business. He hadn't been in-country long enough to decide that there was something weirdly unserious about the whole war. Nobody at the Pentagon had seemed to know or care anything about the invisible airplanes. Two weeks earlier an Undersecretary of Defense had called Lehrner's boss from Washington and asked for someone official to go do something symbolic about the headlines appearing across the country. Before that, nobody had given a goddam about... about whatever they now seemed to care about.

"The world is full of lunatics," Lehrner's boss had muttered dispiritedly to himself, holding the receiver away from his ear with a persecuted expression. "But why do they have to call me?"

"Perhawps you haven't seen the papers," said the cultivated Ivy League voice from the capital, a voice obviously sheathed in an expensive suit and awaiting its opportunity to advance to a full Secretaryship.

"I try not to."

"Ah. Haha. A wit. Well. The Pentagon has come under, ah, pressure from Congress about stories in the AP regarding, um, certain invisible airplanes that seem to be, um, making trouble of a military sort. The Secretary of Defense, a very busy man, wants you to send someone to, um, study the problem."

"Invisible airplanes are impossible," said Lehrner's boss. "There ain't any. How's that for a study?"

"Not good enough, I'm afraid," said the voice, managing to apologize and condescend at the same time. "The Secretary is not interested in their existence, but in having them studied."

"How do you study something when there ain't any?"

The distant expensive suit thought briefly.

"Perhawps by setting up instruments. By taking notes. Perhwaps you could, ah, measure some things. You know, wavelengths and things like that. Perhaps you could do it for, er...about three months? Remember, General Dynamics has a contract coming up...."

Hearn nearly wrecked the jeep dodging a small girl who chased a scrawny chicken into the road. When he had backed and filled and gotten back on the road, Colonel Walther said, "Corporal Hearn has seen the invisible airplanes, gentlemen. Perhaps, Corporal Hearn, you could brief our guests on the threat."

"Lots of 'em," said Hearn. "Bunches." He enjoyed his position as an authority on invisible airplanes. In fact, he regarded himself as the combined Orville and Wilbur Wright of invisible airplanes.

"How many of these alleged airplanes have been sighted?" asked Lehrner sardonically, wondering what the hell was going on.

"None of them, sir," said Hearn.

What? Lehrner corrected himself. The kid was right. These were, after all, invisible airplanes. "I mean, how many of them haven't been sighted?"

"All of them, sir. All of them haven't been sighted, sir." Hearn peered down the road like a bespectacled beagle, looking for mines.

Lehrner grinned. A patch of sanity, this fellow was. He tried again.

"How can you tell when you haven't sighted one?"

"Because you can't see them, sir. When you can't see them least, they're there the most."

"Hmmm," said Potter, whose extra flesh made him quite comfortable in a bouncing jeep. He was gratified that he had been right: Vietnam was an amusing place. "You are saying that their thereness is proportional to their absence. Then it follows that, when you see them most, they must be least there."

"Yessir, that's sort of how they are. Or aren't."

"So if you could make them completely visible, they'd disappear entirely."

"That's what I think, sir," said Hearn. These guys were fun, just like the fellows in his old dormitory.

"Then the solution would seem to be to find where they are, because then they won't be. It should be possible."

Walther almost forgot his dignity. His brow was furrowed with effort. "Wait. Wait," he erupted. "I think I see...You're right! You know, why didn't I think of that? It's so obvious."

"You get a knack for it after a while," said Lehrner. "What else haven't you observed about these planes, Corporal? Aren't they jets, or aren't they helicopters?"

"I figure they aren't jets, or they wouldn't maneuver so fast," offered Hearn.

"Or," said Potter meditatively, "Maybe they aren't something entirely different. There are many things they might not be."

Colonel Walther gasped. "You mean something ...we don't know about? Something—advanced?"

"Almost assuredly something we don't know about, I should think. Practically by definition," said Potter. His vast forehead was beading with moisture. It itched.

"Actually," said Hearn, wondering how much he could get away with, "I met a corporal who said he saw one near China Beach, and it went "eeeee." Real high-pitched."

"Eeeee?" said Colonel Walther.

"Like an L-pad dihedral Eddington oscillator," offered Hearn experimentally.

"Wow!" said Lehrner. That was gibberish, absolute gibberish. He liked this kid.

"Where did you go to school, corporal?"

"Iowa, sir. Chemistry."

"Obviously you were an able student," Potter said. "I'm surprised the marines don't make you responsible for the invisible-airplane investigation. If you aren't already responsible for it, as I begin to think."

The jeep had been climbing steeply. Now it ground to a stop

outside the sandbagged entrance to the Monkey Mountain Hawk sites. Vietnam stretched away below them in luminous veridian and brown, lovely, frightened, and unsure what was happening to it. The Marines who clinked about in the residual mud of the rainy season were not lovely, but they also were brown and green and didn't know what was happening to them. They didn't care as long as they didn't get shot. To one side a battery of sleek Hawk anti-aircraft missiles stood ready to shoot down airplanes the enemy didn't have. The site commander, an angular major with a wad of tobacco in his cheek, came out to see who was intruding on his life this time. Walther leaped from the jeep and spoke briskly.

"Major Minter, these are the experts from General Dynamics. They want to talk to you and your men about the invisible airplanes that are worrying us all and endangering the common soldier. They already have some ideas."

"Why, Ah'm delighted," said the Tennessee-born battery commander sourly. He was not delighted at all. He was getting sick of this invisible airplane business. "Come right in."

Lehrner hesitated. Colonel Walther made him uneasy. The major on the other hand looked to be in his right mind. On impulse he said, "Uh, Dick, why don't you and the colonel keep an eye on the air space while I take a look at the equipment? That way, if anything happens, we've got our bases covered."

"Anything to help," said Colonel Walther dynamically. "The general is very concerned. He worries that one of these mysteriouis planes might kill a common soldier."

Lehrner and the major stepped into a bunker filled with perfectly ordinary radar screens of sorts familiar to both men.

"Major, level with me. What's this crazy bullshit?"

The major propped himself in an angular column against a radio-frequency amplifier, leaned over to spit copiously in a trash can, and picked at his front tooth for a moment. His lean face fell into the expression of sardonic helplessness in the face of cosmically mandated lunacy.

"Jest what you said. Crazy bullshit. There ain't no fucken airplanes. This here's good radar. Ah've been in radar seven years, and Ah know." He spoke in an agonizingly deliberate drawl, as if dictating to a stone cutter. "There cain't be no airplane on high elevation out of clutter that I cain't see."

"Yeah, I know. But something's got everybody upset. We're here because the Pentagon is bent out of shape."

"What it is, some fucken pilot comes out and Ah guess practices fighten, or maybe he's a goddam commonist and hates my guts and jest wants me to answer a lot of damn fool calls from that brainlocked colonel out there that acts like a queer." He meant Walther. "It's a F-4, that's all it is. Dives and rolls and all that good shit. Fucken Air Force don't know who he is, or won't say, or probably don't care."

"Can you get him on radio?"

"He don't answer. Me, I reckon he's crazy. Probably buck nekkid and wearing a goddam red scarf and gigglin' and all."

Lehrner was thinking. "I think I'm supposed to come back with some kind of solution. But there's no problem. Great."

"If I get about one more phone call from that dumb colonel, I'm gonna put me a fire-control solution on that F-4 and drive a Hawk up his ass. Then there won't be no problem."

"Damn. Potter an I gotta come up with something."

"If I was you, Mister, I'd catch me a hop to Bangkok and get me about two week's worth of poontang and hangovers, and then I'd tell the Pentagon the fucken sitchyation needs more study. Then they'll send some other poor sonofabitch and then it's his problem. I know. I used to work at the Pentagon."

"Is the military always this nuts?"

"Yep."

"Then why are you here?"

"Everbody gotta be somewhere."

The sergeant at the search screen hollered, "Major, here he comes now."

"Oh hot dawg," said the major laconically. "That's just fucken peaches. You wanta see a invisible airplane? There he is."

Out over the paddies a dot circled briefly at high altitude, and then plunged toward the earth. It then twisted violently, leading the Major to say, "He's gonna pull a wing off that sucker. Be a good thing too."

Colonel Walther watched in fascination. Why, sure enough, the other plane really was invisible. Some heroic Air Force pilot was fighting an invisible foe. It was splendid.

High over the paddies Major Egglesby was turning hard, watching Togo Fuji grow inexorably in his windscreen.

ANESTHESIA TO THE FORE

Corporal Anesthesia Remingham, a gorgeous specimen of black Alabama manhood at its hopping-maddest, washed his truck at the water point outside the amtrac compound and mourned his pearl-handled forty-fives. Colonel Droningkeit had said they weren't regulation. Anesthesia was overcome by a sense of abused virtue.

"Damn! Whuffo dem wide pcoples take way ma pieces? What I do wrong? Hoo! Black man cain't do nuthin' without some wide muhfuggen colonel be taken way his piece. What dat muhfuh think this is, anyway? A wah zone or a Gal Scout pignick? Hoo! Sumbitch"

Those pistols had for months been the apple of his eye, made especially for him by a shell-carver he found in Bangkok on R-and-R, right next to Linda's Surprise Bar. On one handle of each was a nude and implausibly mammalian girl, almost a double-barreled cow. On the other was inscribed USMCS, universally understood to mean "United States Marine Corps Sucks."

Anesthesia loved those pistols. They were beautiful. They expressed his philosophy. He swaggered with them on his daily runs in his six-by to get water for the Viet Cong training camp, and wore them to the mess hall. They added a little style, he figured, to a camouflage-colored existence. And now that got-dam colonel had made him turn them in to the armorer to be restored to their ugly olive-drab.

He kicked the tire of his truck, to which river mud stuck in great globs, and fussed mightily to himself.

"Shee-it. What I doin' wif dis damn truck anyway? Dat got-dam 'cruiter say I goan be a bummer pilot, go drop bums on de Russians. Dis truck look like a fuggen bummer? Any Russians runnin' roun' here? Sumbitch done lie like a rug . Where my airplane? I goan kill his ass. I goan kick it cross hell and halfa Georgia. Take away my bummer, and take away my piece, Shee-it."

He sprayed the back wheels to loosen the mud, still cursing. Anesthesia did not perhaps have the perfect Marine attitude. Of course, no Marine who was worth a damn ever did. In fact, Anesthesia's background was not designed to give him the right attitude about much of anything . Even his name gave him a had attitude. One reason he liked his pistols was that people were starting to call him Pearl instead of Pain Killer, which appellation he had acquired at Parris Island.

He had originally been named Anesthesia by virtue of being born informally and haphazardly in Montgomery with the assistance of the state police, used in the slums of the South as a sort of low-income obstetrical service. If they didn't know obstetrics, people figured, at least they were cheap. At the time Anesthesia's mother lived in a one-bedroom apartment in a decaying brick building with a leaky roof and paper peeling in mouldering strips from the walls. His father, she thought, might have lived in any of a dozen places, depending on who he was.

The delivery had been complicated. Mrs. Remingham unfortunately had gone into labor after being hit on the head with a marble ashtray by the landlady, who believed that forceful expression was most productive of rent from people who didn't have any money. The cops had duly arrived and delivered the child. The sergeant who filled out the birth-certificate application could not very well ask the unconscious mother what name she had chosen for her offspring. He decided that Anesthesia had a ring to it.

This sort of christening apparently had been going on for years. There was a girl of thirteen next door named Gynecology Ether Dinwiddy.

Anesthesia still didn't know who his father was, but figured that his father didn't know who he was either, which evened things up.

The truck gradually appeared from within its encrustation of glop. The water cut big chunks of goopy mud from the wheels and then rattled against a. 50-cal. ammo box on the truck bed. From within came a disturbed scurrying and scuffling. The box contained a bedraggled rat Anesthesia had found eating the remains of a sandwich he had left there. By closing the top, Anesthesia had become proprietor of the rat. The burdens of ownership were beginning to weigh on him.

"Shee-it. Whut I goan do wif a muhfuggen rat? Guess what, Rat? I ain't got a clue. Maybe I stick a eagle on yo' ass, make you a colonel. Hoo. Be better^n'nat muhfuh we got. Probly smarter. Dat colonel be dumb, 'bout like a pile water buffalo shit. Muhfuh cain` t even fix a car brater. How he goan win no wah° Shee-it."

Anesthesia's ability to fix carburetors was the source of his current discontent. He was a man of high and instinctive mechanical gifts, being able to repair almost anything wit a screw driver, vice-grips, and bits and pieces from a C-ration box. Talent is a dangerous thing. He had recently found Colonel Droningkeit and his driver stalled on the road to Red Beach, puzzled.

"Whuss goin awn sir?" Anesthesia had said.

"Well, sergeant, it seems as if we have a mechanical malfunction," the colonel said a bit stiffly. Talking to sergeants made him uneasy.

"Yassuh. Lemme look. Maybe I fix its butt," said anesthesia, diving under the hood.

Anesthesia had unjammed the butterfly valve with a plastic C-ration fork and a slightly lordly air. It was Anesthesia's view that the ability to repair engines was the best measure suitability for high position.

Unfortunately the colonel had noticed his pistols and checked the regulations. The pistols had been forbidden.

Anesthesia finished washing his truck and drove off to the gas point, still muttering. "Fuggen Patton had'em. Why cain't I? Whut so fuggen special 'bout Patton? Just some wide-ass general. Got lots'em. Too damn many, I say. It's hell. I spozed to git a nukeyouler bummer, and what I gets? A got-dam rat. An' no piece to shoot it with. Shee-it."

GROMMETT ON DUTY

General Grommett squinted and twitched his face to the left, the effect
again being that of a man having an embolism. He was working on a
new soldierly scowl. He thought it expressed a more intense resolve
than his old scowl , while hinting at wellsprings of compassion for
the common soldier. He hoped it spoke of keen intelligence behind
the steel of his exterior. He had heard that this year intelligence was
considered a decisive factor in the choice of a Chief of Staff. The
bureaucrats at Defense were always toying with new ideas instead of
heeding the hard-earned lessons of the past.

He sat up straight behind his forward line of props. These
consisted of a teakwood swagger stick with his name in gold leaf,
and a cigarette lighter made from a WWII grenade. There was also a
coffee cup made from an empty C-ration can with an expended fifty-
caliber round for a handle. He thought it expressed his closeness to
the troops. Behind were his rear line of props, including various
diplomas from staff schools and a captured VC battle flag made by
the VC and sold to American troops to make money to finance their
operations.

General Grommett lifted his chin slightly for a look of' command,
pulled his silvering eyebrows together in his mahogany face, and
pursed his lips. Yes, he thought to himself, the new scowl would do
nicely.

Furtively he slipped his right hand inside his uniform jacket. He
rather thought it made him look like Curtis Lemay. Cronkite was
coming to Danang shortly, and General Grommett wanted the visit

to be a Shot in the Arm for his image. The way things were going, he needed one. Those damned invisible airplanes were giving him hives.

The door opened. Colonel Walther stormed dynamically into his office and yelled, "Don't!"

After a second he added "Sir."

"Don't what?" asked General Grommett, who had been too engrossed in the new scowl to notice Walther's entrance.

"Spit, sir. You looked as if you were going to spit. I thought it might mess up your papers or something."

"Colonel Walther, who are you to tell your commanding officer when he may and may not spit?"

"Yessir. I'm sorry sir. I spoke without thinking. I'll wait."

"For what?"

"For you to spit, sir."

General Grommett was nonplussed. He didn't want to spit on his desk. At least, he didn't think he did. Yet somehow he felt trapped into it. Finally he hedged.

"I'm not going to spit now. But as soon as you leave, I am going to spit. I want you to know that. Right on my deslc."

"Yessir."

"Now what the hell do you want?"

"I don't know, sir. You called me."

General Grommett thought. "Oh, so I did...Oh, it's this. There's been another attack on Third Tracs. Same as the last one. From the sound of it, Charlie's brought in a reinforced battalion. Heavy fighting all around the perimeter, and the only thing that saved the position was gunships. Intel doesn't know why they keep concentrating on Third Tracs, but, goddamit, if they overrun them, right outside Danang, you know what the papers will say."

"Yessir. The commies. What kind of body count did we get?"

"Zero, Bill," said General Grommett, unbending a little. "You know how Charlie is. Drags away his dead. He does it to hurt our image, to make us look unsuccessful. They must have lost heavily in a firefight of that size, but Orientals don't respect human life."

"The immoral yellow bastards."

"They're all godless atheists, Bill. If you don't believe in The Man

Upstairs, you don't care who you kill. It's the Almighty who makes the United States strong, who guides our bombs to their targets. That's the lesson for Americans to learn," said General Grommett, grabbing a new sheaf of papers. "Intel, Bill. Look at this. Look here— infiltration routes, suspected enemy concentrations, and probable attacks."

He was almost whispering. "See the pattern?"

"Nossir," said Colonel Walther truthfully.

"They're converging on Au Phuc Dup. Once you see that, it all makes sense. They want to take out our armor, so they'll have a clear shot at Danang, and take the hamlet just when Cronkite gets here. Can you imagine the devastating effect on American public opinion? Insidious, isn't it?"

Colonel Walther slowly raised his face as the light dawned. "And, Colonel, where have the invisible airplanes been sighted?"

Colonel Walther's fingers drummed excitedly on the table. The logic was inescapable.

"Right ...over...Au Phuc Dup."

Why, wondered Colonel Walther, hadn't he thought of it?

"Now, what we have to do, Bill, is beat them to the punch. I want a major sweep run through there next month, and we'll clean them out. A big victory just when Cronkite gets here. Two can play that game, eh, Colonel?"

THE ENGINEERS ARRIVE

The Air Force 707 approached Danang at high altitude to avoid the cloud of F-4s taking off to drop napalm on railroad tracks. Then it corkscrewed down to the airfield to avoid ground fire. Life in Viet Nam, as even the airplanes seemed to know, consisted chiefly of avoiding one thing or another. As the plane taxied up to the passenger terminal, a jeep raced toward it with an American flag fluttering on the bumper. Colonel Billy Joel Walther, press secretary to General Grommett, leaped out and waited while sweating marines put the ramp in place.

"Don't forget proper military courtesy," Walther fussed at his driver. "The Marine Corps will be judged by our actions."

"Yessir," said Corporal Hearn, waiting with helmet, flak jacket, and burgeoning pride. The engineers on the 707 were coming to investigate his very own invisible airplanes, in which he had come to take paternal pleasure. Almost daily he described their endlessly varied exploits to Feinstein, who put them in the paper, which disturbed General Grommett, who alarmed the Pentagon, which was now sending engineers to see Hearn's airplanes, which by their nature could not be seen. Now Hearn got to see the engineers. He was immensely satisfied with his hobby. He regarded himself as an important part of the war effort.

"Wait here," snapped Walther with what he hoped was just the right mixture of authority and cordiality for dealing with enlisted men. He had learned in OCS to regard soldiers as wily but essentially helpless. They could dig holes if told where, and could do mysterious blue-collar things to trucks, but could not be trusted to change their socks. That was what officers were for, he had concluded, to make sure the men changed their socks.

"Yessir," said Hearn, wishing that Walther would cut the crap. He suspected that Walther really wanted him to say, "Yes, Bwana." Hearn had come to the conclusion that officers were essentially helpless, especially this one. Mostly they just told you to change socks when you didn't need to, but they couldn't fix trucks.

The forward door of the 707 opened like an aluminum sepulcher. Two radar engineers from General Dynamics stepped blinking into the sunlight, wearing blue jeans and fruit boots. Colonel Walther frowned with sudden disapproval. They looked like hippies or dangerous dissidents, or maybe even godless atheists. Perhaps there was some mistake.

Mark Lehrner was a tall rangy engineer with the luxuriant red-brown mustache of a Mexican bandido and a great hawkish ski-slope of a nose. He peered around him with the sardonic curiosity of a sane man forced to visit an asylum. In fact, this was precisely how he regarded himself. His companion, Dick Potter, was rounded and pink with his hair receding from a forehead that looked like an incompletely evolved beachball. There was something haphazard and undisciplined about the pair, something profoundly unmilitary. Colonel Walther decided to request that they not set a Bad Example for the men.

"This is it, John Wayne. Keep your head down. Don't fire until you see the whites of their eyes," Lehrner said in a staccatto Jersey accent. He pulled his head down low under a floppy duck-hunting hat. Lehrner was fundamentally unimpressed by everything except good engineering. He surveyed the sprawling haze-enshrouded expanse of Vietnam, all bright greens fading to misty blues in the distance.

Potter looked calmly around. He too suspected that he had arrived in a vast peninsular looney bin, but he also suspected it would be amusing. The officious man waving his arms by the jeep had potential, he decided.

"It looks as if that guy with the cretinous grin is waiting for us," said Potter. "At least, I'm afraid he is."

"Yep."

"Answer me, Lehrner. Are we really here to look for invisible airplanes?"

"No shit, Kemo Sabe."

They clattered down the steps. "Hello, gentlemen!" said Walther with a firm military handshake. This consisted in slapping the other's hand as if swatting a ping-pong ball and squeezing firmly, like a machine tool. He had seen it done by the Rangers.

"Welcome to Danang, Republic of Viet Nam. We can take groundfire so do put on the flak jackets in the jeep. The ride to Monkey Mountain takes about half an hour. As you know, General Grommett regards your mission with highest priority. He is very worried that these mysterious airplanes may be threatening the common soldier. As you may have read in the media, the General is deeply concerned with the welfare of the common soldier. The general would like to see you afterwards and...."

"Goddam pretty scenery," said Lehrner as they scrambled into the jeep. He found it hard to focus on what Walther was saying, if anything. The metal of the jeep was so hot it was painful to touch. He was looking at Marble Mountain rising in the distance like a square green thumb.

"...of course, we'll provide you with all assistance needed to accomplish your mission and...."

It was not hard to ignore Walther. In fact, it was hard not to ignore Walther..

"That lumpish grey object would seem to be a water buffalo," said Potter. "I didn't think they really existed. What's a buffalo doing on an air base? Do you suppose we're training them to fly?"

Lehrner said, "That one is eating and defecating. Simultaneously."

Colonel Walther stopped talking for a moment. Eating and....? He began to suspect that Lehrner wasn't On The Team. He would have to warn General Grommett.

"Shall I head for Monkey Mountain, sir?" asked Hearn. He liked the newcomers. Only ten minutes in country, and they understood the war.

"Yes, and drive carefully," Colonel Walther replied.

They bounced through countryside peppered with thatched villages, past grey stolid buffalo wondering what it would be like to gore a Caucasian, past wizened mama-sans thinking their unimaginable wizened thoughts, past swarming yellow children yelling "Gimme chop-chop." Lehrner watched the alien landscape with interest, beginning to sweat beneath the luxurious overhang of his moustache. He wondered what the United States thought it was doing here. He also wondered what he himself was doing here. Lehrner had a low tolerance for fools. He had a strong premonition that he had encountered one in Colonel Walther. Something was wrong, he thought. But what? This invisible airplane business was embarrassing. The United States was far ahead of the Soviets in radar, and if Lehrner had no idea how to make an invisible airplane, neither did Ivan.

Besides, there was something weirdly unserious about the whole business. He hadn't been in-country long enough to decide that there was something weirdly unserious about the whole war. Nobody at the Pentagon had seemed to know or care anything about the invisible airplanes. Two weeks earlier an Undersecretary of Defense had called Lehrner's boss from Washington and asked for someone official to go do something symbolic about the headlines appearing across the country. Before that, nobody had given a goddam about... about whatever they now seemed to care about.

"The world is full of lunatics," Lehrner's boss had muttered dispiritedly to himself, holding the receiver away from his ear with a persecuted expression. "But why do they have to call me?"

"Perhawps you haven't seen the papers," said the cultivated Ivy League voice from the capital, a voice obviously sheathed in an expensive suit and awaiting its opportunity to advance to a full Secretaryship.

"I try not to."

"Ah. Haha. A wit. Well. The Pentagon has come under, ah, pressure from Congress about stories in the AP regarding, um, certain invisible airplanes that seem to be, um, making trouble of a military sort. The Secretary of Defense, a very busy man, wants you to send someone to, um, study the problem."

"Invisible airplanes are impossible," said Lehrner's boss. "There ain't any. How's that for a study?"

"Not good enough, I'm afraid," said the voice, managing to apologize and condescend at the same time. "The Secretary is not interested in their existence, but in having them studied."

"How do you study something when there ain't any?"

The distant expensive suit thought briefly.

"Perhawps by setting up instruments. By taking notes. Perhwaps you could, ah, measure some things. You know, wavelengths and things like that. Perhaps you could do it for, er...about three months? Remember, General Dynamics has a contract coming up...."

Hearn nearly wrecked the jeep dodging a small girl who chased a scrawny chicken into the road. When he had backed and filled and gotten back on the road, Colonel Walther said, "Corporal Hearn has seen the invisible airplanes, gentlemen. Perhaps, Corporal Hearn, you could brief our guests on the threat."

"Lots of 'em," said Hearn. "Bunches." He enjoyed his position as an authority on invisible airplanes. In fact, he regarded himself as the combined Orville and Wilbur Wright of invisible airplanes.

"How many of these alleged airplanes have been sighted?" asked Lehrner sardonically, wondering what the hell was going on.

"None of them, sir," said Hearn.

What? Lehrner corrected himself. The kid was right. These were, after all, invisible airplanes. "I mean, how many of them haven't been sighted?"

"All of them, sir. All of them haven't been sighted, sir." Hearn peered down the road like a bespectacled beagle, looking for mines.

Lehrner grinned. A patch of sanity, this fellow was. He tried again.

"How can you tell when you haven't sighted one?"

"Because you can't see them, sir. When you can't see them least, they're there the most."

"Hmmm," said Potter, whose extra flesh made him quite comfortable in a bouncing jeep. He was gratified that he had been right: Vietnam was an amusing place. "You are saying that their thereness is proportional to their absence. Then it follows that, when you see them most, they must be least there."

"Yessir, that's sort of how they are. Or aren't."

"So if you could make them completely visible, they'd disappear entirely."

"That's what I think, sir," said Hearn. These guys were fun, just like the fellows in his old dormitory.

"Then the solution would seem to be to find where they are, because then they won't be. It should be possible."

Walther almost forgot his dignity. His brow was furrowed with effort. "Wait. Wait," he erupted. "I think I see...You're right! You know, why didn't I think of that? It's so obvious."

"You get a knack for it after a while," said Lehrner. "What else haven't you observed about these planes, Corporal? Aren't they jets, or aren't they helicopters?"

"I figure they aren't jets, or they wouldn't maneuver so fast," offered Hearn.

"Or," said Potter meditatively, "Maybe they aren't something entirely different. There are many things they might not be."

Colonel Walther gasped. "You mean something ...we don't know about? Something—advanced?"

"Almost assuredly something we don't know about, I should think. Practically by definition," said Potter. His vast forehead was beading with moisture. It itched.

"Actually," said Hearn, wondering how much he could get away with, "I met a corporal who said he saw one near China Beach, and it went "eeeee." Real high-pitched."

"Eeeee?" said Colonel Walther.

"Like an L-pad dihedral Eddington oscillator," offered Hearn experimentally.

"Wow!" said Lehrner. That was gibberish, absolute gibberish. He liked this kid.

"Where did you go to school, corporal?"

"Iowa, sir. Chemistry."

"Obviously you were an able student," Potter said. "I'm surprised the marines don't make you responsible for the invisible-airplane investigation. If you aren't already responsible for it, as I begin to think."

The jeep had been climbing steeply. Now it ground to a stop

outside the sandbagged entrance to the Monkey Mountain Hawk sites. Vietnam stretched away below them in luminous veridian and brown, lovely, frightened, and unsure what was happening to it. The Marines who clinked about in the residual mud of the rainy season were not lovely, but they were brown and green and didn't know what was happening to them. They didn't care as long as they didn't get shot. To one side a battery of sleek Hawk anti-aircraft missiles stood ready to shoot down airplanes the enemy didn't have. The site commander, an angular major with a wad of tobacco in his cheek, came out to see who was intruding on his life this time. Walther leaped from the jeep and spoke briskly.

"Major Minter, these are the experts from General Dynamics. They want to talk to you and your men about the invisible airplanes that are worrying us all and endangering the common soldier. They already have some ideas."

"Why, Ah'm delighted," said the Tennessee-born battery commander sourly. He was not delighted at all. He was getting sick of this invisible airplane business. "Come right in."

Lehrner hesitated. Colonel Walther made him uneasy. The major on the other hand looked to be in his right mind. On impulse he said, "Uh, Dick, why don't you and the colonel keep an eye on the air space while I take a look at the equipment? That way, if anything happens, we've got our bases covered."

"Anything to help," said Colonel Walther dynamically. "The general is very concerned. He worries that one of these mysteriouis planes might kill a common soldier," said Walther.

Lehrner and the major stepped into a bunker filled with perfectly ordinary radar screens of sorts familiar to both men.

"Major, level with me. What's this crazy bullshit?"

The major propped himself in an angular column against a radio-frequency amplifier, leaned over to spit copiously in a trash can, and picked at his front tooth for a moment. His lean face fell into the expression of sardonic helplessness in the face of cosmically mandated lunacy.

"Jest what you said. Crazy bullshit. There ain't no fucken airplanes. This here's good radar. Ah've been in radar seven years, and Ah know." He spoke in an agonizingly deliberate drawl, as if dictating to a stone cutter. "There cain't be no airplane on high elevation out of clutter that I cain't see."

"Yeah, I know. But something's got everybody upset. We're here because the Pentagon is bent out of shape."

"What it is, some fucken pilot comes out and Ah guess practices fighten, or maybe he's a goddam commonist and hates my guts and jest wants me to answer a lot of damn fool calls from that brainlocked colonel out there that acts like a queer." He meant Walther. "It's a F-4, that's all it is. Dives and rolls and all that good shit. Fucken Air Force don't know who he is, or won't say, or probably don't care."

"Can you get him on radio?"

"He don't answer. Me, I reckon he's crazy. Probably buck nekkid and wearing a goddam red scarf and gigglin' and all."

Lehrner was thinking. "I think I'm supposed to come back with some kind of solution. But there's no problem. Great."

"If I get about one more phone call from that dumb colonel, I'm gonna put me a fire-control solution on that F-4 and drive a Hawk up his ass. Then there won't be no problem."

"Damn. Potter an I gotta come up with something."

"If I was you, Mister, I'd catch me a hop to Bangkok and get me about two week's worth of poontang and hangovers, and then I'd tell the Pentagon the fucken sitchyation needs more study. Then they'll send some other poor sonofabitch and then it's his problem. I know. I used to work at the Pentagon."

"Is the military always this nuts?"

"Yep."

"Then why are you here?"

"Everbody gotta be somewhere."

The sergeant at the search screen hollered, "Major, here he comes now."

"Oh hot dawg," said the major laconically. "That's just fucken peaches. You wanta see a invisible airplane? There he is."

Out over the paddies a dot circled briefly at high altitude, and then plunged toward the earth. It then twisted violently, leading the Major to say, "He's gonna pull a wing off that sucker. Be a good thing too."

Colonel Walther watched in fascination. Why, sure enough, the other plane really was invisible. Some heroic Air Force pilot was fighting an invisible foe. It was splendid.

High over the paddies Major Egglesby was turning hard, watching Togo Fuji grow inexorably in his windscreen.

FEINSTEIN HEARS ABOUT THE INVISIBLE AIRPLANES

Zeke Feinstein sat in the press hooch, sweating like a lawn sprinkler and pondering the strange press release from HQ. He had not felt guilty for days, or even worried about being Jewish. This invisible-airplane business was going to get him a Pulitzer. A big story at last, and he had broken it. His parents would be proud, even if he had changed his name. Of course, he suddenly remembered, they wouldn't know, because he had changed his name. Anyway, the trick now was to take the story and run with it while the other reporters were still off balance.

Flies buzzed torpidly around his coffee cup. From outside came the hollow roaring of amtracs preparing to go look for mines. On the television behind him a high-voiced sergeant with Armed Forces Television explained how the war was speeding the economic development of Vietnam.

"...have found that bomb craters have significant potential as fish ponds, bringing wholesome seafood and nutritious protein for the first time to regions of the Republic of Vietnam that...." he squeaked. Feinstein tuned him out.

The release said, "HQ/USMC—General J. Walter Grommett III, Commander I Corps, announced today that reports of strafing by invisible enemy airplanes have been blown out of proportion. The command has been studying the developing situation for months and while considerations of security prevent further elaboration,

Allied control of the air remains virtually complete. The command stresses that no casualties whatsoever have been sustained as a result of strafing by invisible communist airplanes."

"Hmmmmm, cryptic," thought Feinstein. What did it mean? He assumed that it must mean something. The more straightforward explanation, that it had been written by an idiot and meant nothing, didn't occur to him. He had been in country only two months. The release was a virtual admission that the communists really did have invisible airplanes— meaning, he guessed, some clever technical means for countering radar and making them blend with the sky. Or something. He might ask Hearn, who understood technical things.

The squeaky sergeant intoned from the wall, "...nitrogenating the soil. The paddies of Vietnam have been intensively farmed for centuries, and are now nitrogen-poor. Did you know that every molecule of TNT contains three atoms of nitrogen? This is just another example of how democracy benefits...."

Getting to the bottom of the invisible strafers might not be easy. The brass were obviously keeping this one very quiet. How... ?

Then an idea came. It wasn't much of an idea, but it was the only one he had. As he left the hooch the television rattled "...Morale Services Division has engaged Klok Mortuary and The Gadarene Swine, whose hit single Moonlight and Grave Worms has been the smash number...."

Corporal Hearn was sitting in his jeep at the motor pool, reading Theory of Higher Order Reaction Rates. Feinstein asked him, "What would you do for a whole case of Jim Beam?'

Hearn finished his paragraph before looking up. "Slaughter my mother, put nerve gas in the New York subway system, or eat C-rations two days in a row. That do it?"

"I want to fly with one of those guys who dogfight the invisible airplanes."

"No way, GI."

"You find out who the pilots are for me, and that's a bottle. Two bottles. If I get a ride with one of them in a dogfight, you get the rest of the case."

Hearn thought. He knew there weren't any invisible airplanes, but it didn't seem to make any difference to Feinstein. It didn't seem to make any difference to anybody. Maybe it didn't matter. Everybody seemed to profit from nonexistent invisible airplanes. Hearn sort of liked inventing crazy stories about them and then reading them in the newspapers. Feinstein liked writing them. The Marines liked talking about them. Maybe they didn't have to be real. As for finding the mad pilot who did whatever it was he did up there, it couldn't hurt to try.

"I'll keep an ear out. You hear another trac got it?"

"A mine?"

"Yeah. Gooks keep hiding them, we keep finding them. They gotta figure it out sooner or later, you just can't fool the Corps."

"Yeah. Maybe."

An Efficacious Rat

The sun sank into the South China Sea like the yoke of some dreary egg. The hills surrounding Third Tracs took on a smoky and insubstantial quality, as if reconsidering the advisability of existence. The battalion tensed into an uneasy alertness. HQ was expecting a major attack. Colonel Droningkeit doubled the guard, and then sat in his hooch and gazed irritably at an estimate from intelligence. He never could understand the goddammed things. This one seemed to say that there would be an attack, and it seemed to say that there wouldn't be an attack.

Sometimes he wondered whether he was smart enough for this business. Every time he went to the Intel shop, they showed him maps that had the same four VC units listed in four different places. When he asked how this was possible, that Ivy League colonel, Toute or Toupe or something, always said, "But this, you understand, is a topographical map, and this one has little red lines in the corners. See? It takes a while. You get used to it."

Colonel Droningkeit never did.

That night Corporal Hearn and Larry were again atop Old Motherfucker, their duly appointed amtrac, this time with a sandbagged machine gun. Happy Valley stretched black before them, cherry tracers leaping silently in the distance. Corporal Beans was off somewhere in a machine-gun bunker. He pulled a lot of guard duty because guards didn't have to speak English.

"Scared, Hearn?" asked Larry, crouched down behind the raised hatch coaming. He kept his cigarette on the hatch ledge, out of sight, and stuck his head through the hatch to take a drag.

"No. Not really. They won't hit us. They can't afford to."

"What you mean?"

Hearn stared into the blackness of the valley. Mortar flares as usual shivered in the clouds. A few amtracs coughed into life, ready to charge an attacking enemy. They rumbled hollowly in the nervous evening, belching greasy smoke, as safeties clicked off along the wire and searchlights stabbed the night.

"I figure amtracs keep their morale up," said Hearn thoughtfully.

"Bull ...You reckon?"

"Sure. Don't think so? If you were Charlie, wouldn't you like to watch the bad guys driving a thirty-seven ton mine-detector with the gas tank in the bottom? A real giggle. Bet the fucking gooks sell tickets to sit in the mountains in the morning and watch us blow up. You know, like R-and-R. Do a good job, and you get to drink beer, kick hack, and watch a few tracs blow up."

"Oh, hell. You don't really believe that, do you?"

"You don't really disbelieve it, do you?".

Larry thought about it. Yeah, it made sense. Or maybe it didn't. The distinction did not seem as clear as it once had. Hearn pressed his advantage.

"I mean, if you were a dink sapper and risked your ass day after day just to blow up a damn bread truck or something, you'd get discouraged, right? Boom, and nothing but fucking bread crumbs. But if you could watch a P-5 go up, ker-blam, guys running around on fire and great big flames and shit, you'd stay in the war. Just for the hell of it. I figure we're like Bob Hope for the gooks."

Larry retracted his head beneath the sandbag line as a spent bullet fzzzzzzzed overhead. Funny thing about this war, he thought: Most people who got hit weren't being shot at.

"Yeah, shit. Maybe we could show'em a hoochee-coochee show instead. You ever see how crazy a dink goes when he looks at a Playboy? They never seen tits like that."

Forty yards to their left Corporal Beans Lopez waited in the darkness behind the machine gun in his bunker. The air in the bunker was close, the evening muggy. Beans peered at the distant ring of mortar flares through the holes in the sheet of beach matting that hung down from the overhang of the bunker to keep grenades out. It looked like rows and rows of portholes.

Beans understood dimly that he was to shoot anyone who tried to come through the wire. It seemed to him a reasonable thing to do, or at least no more unreasonable than anything else.

Whatever this war was about, a question that still tugged occasionally at his consciousness, it made sense that people had to be shot, or else it wouldn't be a war. He thought about Rosita, his three-year-old sister in Saltillo, and wondered whether he would see her again. Dios, it would be good to watch Rosita chasing through the cholla, all dark eyes and plump churning little legs, and watch the purple dusk come over the desert and......

Something clinked in tie wire. Beans jerked into full alertness. Hijo de la chingada. Someone was out there?

Chinkalink.

Si, indeed. Someone was.

Well then, he, Beans, would shoot the maricon. That was easy. Being a Spanish-speaking Marine in an English-speaking Corps, Beans was happiest on those rare occasions when he knew what he was expected to do. He swiveled the M-60 toward the sound, waited for it to come again, and opened fire.

Braprapraprap. Tracers flew in startling pink brightness and ricocheted crazily from the earth. The noise was terrific.

"Hay Japoneses en el alambre" roared Beans. His understanding of the origins and participants in the war still hazy.

The next bunker quickly opened up, spraying more tracers at the impact point of Beans' tracers. The new bunker didn't know what it was shooting at either, but figured that, whatever it was, it was probably where Beans was shooting. Beans felt confirmed in his judgement that he was being attacked, since the other bunker was shooting the same intruder.

The firefight developed rapidly. Marines in rifle pits added to the din with M-14s. Whooom! A grenade detonated in a violent orange flash.

"Ammo! We need ammo!" came a cry along the line after a few minutes of frantic combat. Daring Marines streaked for the magazines. A hell of an attack was underway. There came the heavy buddha-buddha-buddha of fifty caliber machine guns. Pandemonium reigned. The tracers were almost sheets of electric pink flame.

"Jesus, you see anything?" yelled Larry over the din. He was feeding the machine gun for Hearn. Brass from the gun sprayed from the chamber, clinked against the armor, and fell to the ground.

"Naw! Must be in the bushes, though," roared Hearn, crazily hosing the distant foliage while keeping his head barely above the sandbags. The gun jerked and shook. "Shit! I didn't think they'd really come!"

Fire erupted from bunkers on the other side of the camp as gunners opened up at deep shadows that seemed closer to the perimeter than they had been before. In the commo bunker, Colonel Droninghkeit was calling on the radio, "F'irebase Bravo, Firebase Bravo, this is Dream 35. We are under attack, repeat under heavy attack. Immediate barrage requested along main Happy Valley axis. This is a tactical emergency."

Shortly the boom, roar, and wham of 105s began. Huge orange flashes erupted on the exposed slopes.

"Keep firing!" Colonel Droningkeit screamed, running along the wire to encourage his men. "They can't take this long. Keep up the pressure." He sprinted toward the other side of the camp to check on the progress of the fight.

The battle raged on. Helicopters began to lift off at the airfield, gunships coming to investigate. An AC-130 gunship, a transport made into a mass of guns, began warming up. Third Tracs was in danger of being overrun, the pilot was told on his radio. Charlie had to be stopped. The US couldn't afford to lose this one. The hospitals prepared to minister to mangled casualties that must come, although as yet none had.

Down by the motor pool, Anesthesia sat in the back of his six-by, smoking and listening. He basked in a warm glow of philosophic satisfaction. The original target of the massed firepower of the base, a rat with a beer can tied to its tail, had long since taken shelter in a hole.

"Hoo! Dem wide folks fighten like hell. Pertecten democracy!

Now maybe that muhfuggen colonel get his ass roasted. Man! I done built me a torpedo rat! Shee-it. Invented its ass."

It was the fifth torpedo rat he had dispatched in two weeks, and each had caused a spectacular firefight. He dropped half a sandwich to his new rat in the 50-cal can and lit another cigarette.

A MATTER OF LINGUISTICS

Colonel Max Perdiem, his face coated in grave-mould green-and-black grease paint, peered lethally from beneath the thick foliage at the bottom of a ravine. At least he hoped he was peering lethally. It was hard to tell. He wasn't sure whether his tightly focused squint looked dangerous or just near-sighted.

The forest was dim and sepulchral, the sunlight being absorbed by thick triple-canopy far above. Thick foliage muffled sounds. The rotting vegetation in which he lay was unpleasantly moist. Things crawled in it. He knew that men in Special Operations often had to lie, motionless yet alert, for hours in unpleasant places outdoors. His current circumstances undeniably being unpleasant, he felt a sense of fulfillment. He embodied the military view that soldiers should lead a life of sacrifice and hardship. Sacrifice for what was irrelevant and sometimes confusing. Still, whenever he was comfortable, he had a vague sense that something was wrong.

He could see little in the densely leafy curtain of growth. For three hours he had waited motionless, at times wishing that he had chosen an observation post without an ants' nest. He understood himself to be on a crucially important mission in search of Viet Cong trains, or perhaps of rail crews building them. Colonel Walther hadn't been too clear on the question. The nature of intelligence was not to be clear.

He had reflected that the bottom of a boggy ravine would be an odd place to build a rail line. He also new that surprise was the soul of strategy, and finding a rail line in a ravine too narrow for a box car would indeed be surprising.

A camouflaged radio lay beside him. He very quietly slipped the rubber face piece over his mouth, designed to muffle his voice lst enemies hear him. It made him look like a disturbed horse with a feed bag. He keyed the microphone.

"Wo shang i-hau, da bidz yo da pigu," he whispered and waited for a response in his earphone. He believed that he was speaking Montagnard.

Back came a soft response from Ksor Ksor, his Montagnard second, "Wo hen yao chr dofu. Pi-jyou hau."

Ah, so his team hadn't found any trains either. The Cong must be very, very good, thought Perdiem. Trains were hard to hide. Something wasn't right. After a week of looking for them in a small region, something nagged at him.

He got to his feet and began stealthily moving toward the creek where his 'Yards waited.

Months before, Perdiem had been assigned the three 'Yards of his team. They were small brown men with high cheek bones, of a breed not far removed from the Stone Age, intelligent if blankly ignorant of anything beyond their highland villages, and unsure why the strange Americans were in the jungles. They knew there was a war, though they were not sure why. It didn't occur to them that the white men might not know either. They knew though that no Viet Cong were anywhere near the Annamese Finger.

However, the Special Forces paid them money for walking around in the woods. Money was a new concept to them. It was their understanding that money could be exchanged for motor scooters. All three had ambitions of doing just that. If the Americans wanted them to look for VC who weren't there, they would look for them. Since they couldn't find any, they would keep getting paid for looking. It seemed to them a reasonable or at least desirable arrangement.

From the start Perdiem had addressed them in their Montagnard dialect, which he had been taught at the Defense Language Institute in Monterrey, California. As was usual with military students, he had learned almost nothing, and yet assumed that he was fluent. Everyone knew that Special Forces men were fluent in exotic languages, so he must be.

From this confusion, a curious and portentous sequence of events would flow.

Following his arrival at the Special Forces base camp in the Annamese Finger, Perdiem had begun holding PT sessions in the morning. These struck the Yards as little short of lunacy, but if mental disturbance was the price of motor scooters, as it seemed to be, then they would be disturbed. Nothing else the large white men did made any sense, so why should this?

And so at six in the morning, against a glowing backdrop of emerald-green hills swathed in silver morning fog, on the red scraped clay behind barbed wire of the camp, they jumped up and down and waved their arms curiously as the strange colonel shouted orders. They didn't understand what PT was, but on the other hand they didn't much care. The odd colonel often say something to them in, as he thought, their dialect. They found it incomprehensible. In fact they had no idea what language he was speaking.

"Wo shr-ge ben dan! Dwei-le! Gen syau gou i-yang!" the skull-faced apparition with the jagged lightning scar had shouted. Then he had begun jumping up and down while waving his arms and straddling his legs. The Yards had stared, thunderstruck. They had never seen anything of such surpassing curiousness.

"Fang-pi i! Fang-pi er! Fang-pi san!" shouted Perdiem, furiously fanning the air. Unfamiliar with calisthenics, and not wanting to embarrass him, they had nodded, smiled, and tried to guess what the crazy colonel wanted. Ah. He wanted them to jump and fan the air too. Why? they wondered. Maybe it didn't matter. They began jumping and fanning. A motor scooter was a motor scooter.

Being bright, the Yards had gradually come to associate the sounds Perdiem made with what he was trying to say. Since they didn't recognize his utterances as Montagnard, they were under the impression that he was teaching them another language. They began to answer him in the same words. Soon they were able to communicate quite adequately for purposes of patrolling. He thought he was speaking their language, and they, that he wasn't.

This too would have consequences.

One day the sharp fwopfwopfwop of a helicopter had come from high in the empty blue sky. A resupply bird. It descended like some ugly ill-designed insect, the rotor wash blowing loose trash through the wire, and whined to a stop. The pilot, technically Warrant Officer Reginald F. Houlihan but everywhere known as Six-pack, climbed out with a beer in his hand and a cowboy hat on his head. Things got a little loose away from headquarters.

"Hey, Six-pack, good to see your ass," said one of the SF men, all of whom knew Six-pack well. "You got goodies?"

"Do I got goodies? Twelve pizzas, case of Beam, bag of dirty books," Sixpack said, non-regulation blond hair reaching his collar. He looked like an Irish motorcycle bandit. "You want maybe ammunition or something?"

"Naw. Never use it. Now, about them fucken pizzas…."

Six-pack was so called because he always flew with a copious supply of Vietnamese beer in the cockpit. It wasn't regulation, but neither was Six-pack. Someone at the base camp asked him why the beer. "In twenty-three years in these whirly-birds, I've only crashed twice. Both times I was sober. I'm not going to risk it again."

He met Perdiem, and decided that here was a man, if not exactly after his own heart, at least more interesting than most people he met in Viet Nam. They got along. Six-pack offered to help Perdiem's team as best he could. Perdiem liked night missions as he thought these would catch the enemy off guard. Trains, he thought, might be less alert in the dark. Six-pack was happy to support these missions because he could park in a clearing and be left alone. He knew that there were no VC about. The other Special Forces troops encouraged Six-pack to take Boo Boo away, if only for a night. There was always hope that he might forget how to get back.

The chopper always inserted them in a jungled clearing and then Six-Pack would shut the turbine down and contentedly drink until morning. Theoretically he was standing ready to extract them in case they were in danger of being overwhelmed. Insertion and extraction, thought Muldoon: In like suppositories, and out like teeth. It pretty much defined the military as he understood it.

Night after night, day after day, Perdiem and his team crept through the area of operations. They found nothing, though the colonel fell repeatedly into gullies, quicksand, and arroyos. Something wasn't right with the world. It was almost, Perdiem thought, as if the trains were invisible.

MARKETING DEFENSE

Julius Pierpoint, the marketing director for General Dynamics' Office of Military Systems, peered sternly at Mark Lehrner through ponderous horn-rimmed glasses. Engineers were such wretched nuisances. They never understood marketing. He sometimes wondered why the corporation didn't do away with them. It would facilitate business.

"Listen, Julius," Lehrer was saying with an air of strained patience, "There aren't any invisible airplanes, got it?"

"Aren't any?" Julius Pierpont frowned.

"None. Zip. Zero. Now I don't want to get over your head with technical details, but I think I can convey the essential point. Listen carefully. You can't detect what isn't there. It's a principle of engineering. See? No can do. No plane, no detect. Sorry."

Julius Pierpoint's full lips twitched beneath the looming rims of his glasses, making him look like a swarthy and agitated rabbit. The Pentagon was offering three hundred million green ones for an operational invisible-airplane detector, with the possibility of an unlimited production run for the NATO allies. In fact the Department of Defense had suddenly wakened to a new danger: No invisible airplanes had been detected in Europe, showing that even the sophisticated early warning radars of the Alliance were being fooled.

While America had been sleeping, the Russians had stolen a technological march on the free world. In addition to the Invisible Airplane Gap, there seemed to be a Radar Gap also, and the Pentagon was frantic to acquire equipment to overcome the disadvantage. Such a demanding project could easily run into billions of dollars, especially with the help of General Dynamics' accounting department. And Lehrner was interposing trifling objections.

"I don't understand. Can't you just make a more powerful detector? For $300 million, it should be possible to detect anything. Whether it's there or not."

Lehrner was almost jiggling with frustration. "But you don't understand. These alleged invisible airplanes aren't there." Lehrner stared a Pierpoint with the expression of a man who has just realized that he is talking to a tape recording.

"Ah! I see. Then where are they? We need to make something to find them, and then detect them. Of course, the added capability will add to development costs, heh, hmmm. How long should that take?"

Dick Potter interposed from within the serenity of his pink sphericity, "Three months. Easy."

Pierpoint perked up like a beaver discovering water after a long stretch of desert. "Wonderful! I knew realism would at last come to the fore. Excellent. I'll prepare an announcement." And he hurried out the door.

Lehrner turned to stare at Potter with the expression of a man who has recently been poisoned. Potter smiled as seraphically as Buddha after two martinis.

"Dick, have you lost your alleged mind? That horn-rimmed slime mold is committing us to ...committing...I can't think about it."

"Yes. So we design it."

"How do you detect what isn't there?"

"Amplify."

"What?"

"Listen to me, Mark. We throw something together, you know, a little bit of IR, some stuff from Radio Shack, lots of knobs and blinking lights. Ok? Then we pass it off to some junior guy for full-scale development. It won't work, so we say it needs to be more sensitive. Then we get lots of money to work on really nice high-end IR spectrophotometers. That's where the action is, not in this radar altimetry we're doing. And of course it won't hurt us to be design leaders on a $300 million project."

"I can't believe we're doing this."

"Wait a few years."

A Distant Puppeteer

In his bungalow outside Clark Air Force Base in the Philippines, Lieutenant Gopher J. Trilling pawed through his refrigerator with broad stubby hands like paddles. Then he shoved into his mouth, underslung beneath the long pyramidal protuberance of his nose— an imposing and improbable organ that blended like a ski slope sunk into his forehead—an artichoke-and-mayonnaise sandwich from which excess mayonnaise dropped in globs. Then he flung himself into a stuffed chair and began peering through thick glasses at the Wall Street Journal. Then he smiled the warm, glowing smile of a desert father who has just had breakfast with God. This was Lieutenant Trilling's response to money. McDonnell Douglass had gone up four points.

On the walls, lizards copulated vigorously with little cries of, "Urk! Urk!" He didn't notice the lizards.

Nobody suspected that he was the richest man in the Air Force. In fact, almost nobody noticed that he existed. Lieutenant Trilling was, except for his proboscis and his inexplicable understanding of the stock market, perhaps the most nondescript man in the Air Force. He seemed to have no characteristics. He didn't date. He was neither brave nor cowardly. Nobody liked or disliked him. Except for artichoke-and-mayonnaise sandwiches, heavy on the mayonnaise, he seemed to like nothing. Or to dislike it. It was true that he looked very much like a mole, which made some of the wives nervous when he walked past their lawns, but it was nothing they could put a finger on.

Every day he went to the Office of Personnel, Housing, and Inclement Statistics, where he was in charge of maintaining records. His purpose in the great scheme of the Air Force was to manage a wall lined with filing cabinets. These contained forms dealing with nobody knew what, since no one ever looked at them except the pool of eight Philippino secretaries who filled them out in large numbers. Someone had once known what the forms dealt with, but he had been transferred to Europe and, since things were running smoothly, nobody had ever inquired again. If it ain't broke, the Air Force felt, don't fix it.

The filing system never broke, because Lieutenant Trilling was a good manager. When the cabinets filled, he emptied the last cabinet into the Dempster Dumpster late at night, and moved the empty cabinet to the front of the row of cabinets. When the new cabinet filled, he emptied the current last cabinet into the Dumpster. The Philippino secretaries were grateful because they always knew where to put their forms. However, it had the effect of causing the cabinets gradually to migrate around the walls.

This puzzled his boss, Major Dornington, who had a vague feeling that the furniture in his offices was up to something.

"Lieutenant Trilling," he occasionally asked, "Wasn't... I mean, wasn't this filing cabinet somewhere else yesterday?"

Lieutenant Trilling always answered this question in the tones of one soothing the disturbed, "Everything was always somewhere else yesterday, sir. The planet circles the sun and the galaxy moves through space. We're always somewhere else."

"Ah, that must be it. I knew it was somewhere else yesterday." Major Dornington was pleased that he wasn't imagining things.

By midsummer however the cabinets had reached the desk of the first Philippino secretary, which faced the wall. Lieutenant Trilling moved her desk along the wall by the width of a filing cabinet, and pushed the other seven desks down by the same amount. Soon the office was being orbited by eleven filing cabinets, eight Philippino secretaries, a magazine stand, and a portable water cooler. Major Dornington became vaguely anxious and began to dream of being trapped in whirlpools.

"Lieutenant, do you notice anything odd about the furniture?

"No sir," answered Lieutenant Trilling. ""It looks pretty ordinary to me."

"Ah...Then you don't have a suspicion that it's ...you know ...trying to get behind you?"

"No, sir," Four Eyes said in a voice tinged by concern.

Major Dornington didn't answer. He did begin turning his desk so that it always faced the migrating cabinets.

Lieutenant Four-Eyes Trilling had gotten rich after inheriting ten thousand dollars from his great aunt Placenta. When Four Eyes inherited the ten thousand from his aunt, he put it in the bank. He didn't have any particular need for money, and he was content watching his cabinets migrate around the edge of the office, which seemed about as reasonable as anything else people did.

He had then begun casually reading the Wall Street Journal, and discovered that he had an eye—an astonishingly good eye, as it turned out—for stocks. Further, found that he loved stocks. They were fun. Few things were. Soon he was making money hand over fist, rolling in lucre almost, and loving every penny of it with the affection of a boy for his cocker spaniel. His telephone bills to his broker in New York were large, but paled beside his earnings.

This fiscal flowering had its drawbacks, mostly involving taxes. A man making eighty thousand a year plus a lieutenant's salary, he learned, is vulnerable tax-wise. He began to cast about for shelters, and discovered that anyone in a combat zone could take a tax credit of $2000. It was a law designed to benefit officers. He also found that supply flights went from the Philippines to Bangkok every month, flying over Vietna briefly. By flying six times a year, he could get twelve months of credit, or $24,000. It helped that he was in charge of the records.

He was making so much money however that $24,000 wasn't enough. He began making a twofer flight every month, which gave him twelve thousand in credits and twenty-four months per year of combat flying. For a while he wondered whether the computer would object to his existing at twice the normal rate, but it didn't. The Air Force just wasn't set up for people who lived twenty-four months a year.

Still his earnings outran his tax credits. He found that if he stayed

in Bangkok overnight, and flew back over Vietnam en route ho e
on the first of the months, he could file for his credits through Off tt
Air Force Base in Oklahoma, on the other side of the Internatio al
Date Line, where it was still the thirty-first. This doubled his cre ts
to twenty-four thousand, but gave him combat time at the rate of
forty-eight months per year.

Normally a lieutenant would not have been permitted to m ke
long flights to Bangkok every month. However, Major Dorning n
was concerned about his mental balance, and Lieutenant Trill g
assured him that he wasn't crazy. Several times a month Ma r
Dornington asked about the galaxy and how things were ne er
where they were. It comforted him, so he left Lieutenant Wimb y
pretty much free to do as he liked.

FEINSTEIN FLIES

On the day of Feinstein's flight with Major Egglesby, the sun came up without hitch and began as usual to fry the brains of anyone foolish enough to be in Vietnam. Anesthesia woke early to feed a huge new torpedo rat he had acquired, now in training. General Grommett sat in his office, between his forward and rear props, and considered a plan to use cargo planes as bombers and thus get his numbers up. On AFARTS the squeaky-voiced corporal piped that discarded brass shell-casings were providing Viet Nam with a priceless industrial resource for the manufacture of ash trays, Viet Nam's largest manufacture since the rice had been mostly poisoned by defoliants.

As the mist burned off the paddies, the eleven-year-old agents sallied forth from hooches to sell boom-boom, and thousands of American soldiers walked around in the ghastly heat, as if they were part of a sane enterprise. Amtracs blew up with thunderous explosions as they found mines. Everything was as it always was, and apparently always would be, bureaucracy without end. That was the day Feinstein's head got too heavy.

Hearn appeared in his jeep at Feinstein's hooch to take him to the air field. When Feinstein struggled out, Hearn was sitting in the jeep with his legs propped over the steering wheel and reading Stochastic Methods in Multivariate Polymer Analysis.

"Hearn, that shit's qotta soften your brain. You read it?"

"If I didn't, who would?" asked Hearn, a master of the irrefutable question.

"I give up."

Feinstein hated chemistry. He was already beginning to sweat, the drops leaving a trail of fine matted hair as they rolled down his arms. Feinstein decided he hated weather too, not any particular weather, but just weather.

"Nervous?" asked Hearn as he drove off toward the gate.

"Who, me? No. I always shake in the morning. It's the best time."

Hearn's round face turned briefly toward Feinstein and he said, "I wouldn't worry. I hear they're pretty sure they've fixed whatever made the wings come off that F-4 over Phu Bai, and..."

"Stop it!" screamed Feinstein, who secretly believed that all airplanes were waiting to disintegrate the moment they got him to a fatal altitude. He was no longer sure he wanted to go with a certified maniac in pursuit of whatever Major Egglesby pursued. At the gate the swarm of spindly pimps began yelling of their wares. "Jesus, selling their sisters. Sorta turns your stomach, doesn't it?" said Feinstein.

"I figure it's like a paper route. Listen, I hope you told someone to give me my bourbon if you don't come back. You know, like a last will and testament...."

"Shut up, goddamit. That's not funny."

"I know. It's real serious. A whole case."

At the ready room Feinstein hopped out and began to feel inadequate. He always felt inadequate around pilots. He knew he looked like an elongated tarsier with hair on his ear lobes. He was pretty sure these lugubriously masculine fighter jocks thought he was ridiculous. While he was worrying, a tall lantern jawed private named Dooley took him in tow. Hearn drove off, pleased with the way his war was going. He had never dreamed how easy it was to run a war. It still amazed him. You just told stories to reporters, and Congress did spasmodically irrelevant but endlessly amusing things.

Before coming to Vietnam he had had no idea the world worked in such a crazy way. It made him think of his patented rule for answering essays questions in college: On every third question, choose an absurd answer and argue for it cogently. Then you got credit for independence of thought.

If you had to spend thirteen months in this chemically

uninteresting waste, you might as well shape international history. That's how Hearn looked at it.

The tall private wore thick glasses like portholes in an unusually capacious gourd. He spoke in a mournful uninflected monotone that didn't stop for sentence endings.

"Sir. Good morning sir," he droned, "I'm Private Dooley and if you'll just follow me I'll brief you for your flight sir." He then waited for a response, peering glassily down at Feinstein as if he had just stimulated a new and interesting bug and wanted to see what it would do. This was not far from the case. Dooley regarded the Air Force as utterly amazing. He derived unending entertainment from watching to see what it would do next.

"Yeah, sure. What do I gotta do?"

Feinstein considered Dooley and decided he looked like the forequarters of a robust but chronically disoriented giraffe.

"Yes sir I have to tell you the emergency procedures sir in case anything goes wrong which it probably won't but you never can tell especially in heavy ground fire and these worn-out airplanes."

When Dooley ended a sentence, or rather an oration, he did it with such finality that Feinstein felt that he ought to put a coin in a slot to hear what came next. They came to the briefing room. Long rows of dark green helmets lined the shelves like mouldering forgotten heads.

"What procedures?"

"Yes sir if you have to bail out you ought to put your head back so the ejection motor won't crush you vertebra and then pull these striped handles but if you get nervous in flight don't grab them for security because you won't get any and keep your legs close to your body or they'll hit the instrument panel and tear off."

Feinstein eyed the myriad of ominous gauges and screens in the cockpit. Then he eyed Dooley. Next he thought of himself with his legs torn off. Then he wondered why he hadn't become a stock broker. Stock brokers sometimes jumped from skyscrapers, but their chairs never shot into the air with them and crushed their vertebrae.

Dooley's voice droned down from between his huge globular lenses. "If you eject at an altitude of more than ten thousand feet your parachute won't open because there's not enough oxygen at ten thousand feet and you might have brain damage so don't worry and just wait until you get to ten thousand feet and it opens and if it doesn't then you better think of something to do although I'm not sure what but it's a problem that doesn't last real long and...."

Feinstein struggled to picture it. This military shit was fundamentally weird, unsound. At thirty thousand feet the cockpit fills with acrid black smoke, he thought. I lean my head back so my vertebrae don't crush and, foomp! I squirt out like a goddam pop tart, and there I am hanging in fucking giddy space with no airplane and starting to..urg...fal-ll-ll. Yes, that makes sense. Keep calm, says this bug-eyed lunatic.

"Dooley, this is crazy. It's diseased."

"Yes sir but it's the Air Force and I go home next month anyway."

A door opened and a handsome blond in a flight suit strode in. His hair rose in a crest and his chin pointed in two directions at once. Feinstein stared at him, never having seen anything so gorgeous or deformed. This guy looks like a slingshot, he thought. Or some kind of tropical bird.

"Ah, the minion of the Fourth Estate, ready for a little air combat, eh? P

lay the Big Game? Nothing like it!"

He shook Feinstein's hand with a steely grip that had once thrown long hopeless passes for the Tuskaweegee Bruins and slapped him on the back. His blue eyes sparkled with courage and zest and confusion. Feinstein stared into those empty pools and thought, hmmm, nice house but no furniture. The lights were on but nobody was home.

"Well, Major, it's a big story and we minions ...you know, anything to get the story."

"Anything for the mission, eh? Hey, I like that."

"Uh, Major, level with me. Do these invisible airplanes, you know, exist?"

Major Egglesby gazed at him from between the golden tidal wave of hair and his magnificent chin. He found the question somehow confusing. Probably it was in bad taste to have asked it. To tell the truth, Major Egglesby was no longer entirely sure about the invisible airplanes.

He had been sure they didn't exist until his interview with Colonel Dravidian. Now, however, they existed, as a matter of Air Force policy. But then, where had they come from? There was something puzzling about it all.

"Certainly they exist."

"How do you know?"

"Because those are my orders. Obedience to orders is a martial virtue. You have a lot to learn about the military way. I can see that, my good man. It's a cleaner, nobler way of life, but there are sacrifices."

"Your orders are to tell me they exist?" asked Feinstein, groping for something he could get hold of.

"No. My orders are that they do exist. I don't have any orders about what to tell you."

A loon, thought Feinstein. What entertainment. He was putting his life in the hands of a scatter-brained airborne Beowulf.

On the runway, in air shimmering with little squiggles of heat, he proceeded to strap himself into the wizzo's seat. He found it unsettling. There was a great sea of writhing green belts and harness, all with different and puzzling buckles. Most were ingeniously designed to snap painfully shut on his thumbnail, although a few pinched his fingers as he jammed one part into another. Within moments he began to feel as though he were being engulfed by some insidious nylon octopus. He wondered why he was doing this. The wings would come off, he was sure of it.

Major Egglesby watched his spiderish passenger and thought of the Good, the True, and the Warlike. He was pleased with the importance of his mission, pleased he had after all gotten to the heart of the great Southeast Asian combat. He was fighting the invisible airplanes of a devious foe. He was glad he had been wrong about their not existing. He attributed his discovery of them to the essentially warlike instincts of his soul. He would soon be an Ace, Colonel Dravidian had implied. He smiled a smile tinged with doom.

The canopy slammed closed and sealed with a sepulchral thump. Oh god, I'm going to drown, thought Feinstein. Then came a whine and the big engines began to howl mournfully.

"Eh? What's that noise?" said Major Egglesby over the intercom.

Feinstein realized that he had begun to howl mournfully himself. He stopped.

"Guess it's nothing. All right, let's roll! Up and at'em! Roll the dice with fate, yank and bank, back for lunch with our comrades in arms! Ah, that's the life. And if one day you don't come back? Who lives forever?"

Major Egglesby rammed the throttles home. The squat fighter lumbered forward. A weight pushed against Feinstein's chest. The air field began to roll past, faster and faster. Jesus, Feinstein thought, how can anything anything as big as South Vietnam accelerate so fast?

He peered blankly down at the receding earth, a frail, hairy, hawk-nosed bundle of distress, and began to moan quietly to himself. Fear had nothing to do with it, although he was afraid. He was offended in a deep and inconsolable way by the sheer unreasonableness of things. Only a few years before he had been a normal kid in East Hoboken, groping at Mary Jenkins in the overgrown weeds behind Marzrati's Chevrolet and worrying only about transient acne.

Now here he was, flying off to do battle with airplanes that apparently didn't exist, for which he would almost certainly win a Pulitzer Prize. It was crazy. He had invented these immaterial craft, when he thought they did exist, and now, when he thought they didn't, he was going to win a Pulitzer for discovering them. He had tried to explain to his editor in New York, but without success.

"Don't exist?" Murphy had roared over a staticky line from New York. "You bet your sweet ass they exist. Eleven hundred and twenty-three column inches we've run on those goddam airplanes, and you say they don't exist? They exist, goddamit. That's company policy."

"But that's lying."

"What you think this is? A fucken high-brow monthly? Can you prove they don't exist?"

"Well, no."

"Then they might exist, right? Whaddya want, for Christ's sake? Godlike certainty?"

They reached thirty thousand feet and circled in the high crystalline world of altitude, bathed by intense sunlight. Over his own moaning, Feinstein heard the engines howling like great unhappy vacuum cleaners. Witches ride brooms, he thought, but I ride vacuum cleaners. He was beginning to feel nauseated by the turns. The oxygen mask gripped his face with a clammy feel, which didn't help his gut. The hose was attached like a crimped worm. The oxygen flowed, "Sssssssss....ehhhhhhhhhhhh," and his voice sounded hollow and impersonal, like an asthmatic on Quaaludes. The green table of Vietnam sprawled below, riding out yet another incomprehensible war. It was used to it.

Major Egglesby also was puzzled, and for once knew it. He peered with the eyes of a great hunting bird into the arching blue dome of the sky, wondering what to do. The Air Force, he decided, was more mystifying than he had thought. Before, when the invisible airplanes didn't exist, he had known how to fight them. Now that they existed, he wasn't sure how to proceed. How could he tell when one was out there? He decided to do as he had always done. Everyone seemed happy with it.

"There they are!" he shouted. "Bandits! Ten o'clock low!"

"Where?" said Feinstein, looking hard but seeing nothing. He wasn't quite sure where ten o'clock was.

"Low! They're sneaking in to bomb the orphanage! My god, it's Togo Fuji himself!"

Major Egglesby assumed that Colonel Togo Fuji lived chiefly from a fiendish hatred of orphans, whom he cherished as being necessary to the practice of swordsmanship. He wasn't sure whether it was Air Force policy that Togo Fuji existed, as Colonel Dravidian had said nothing of it. Maybe it was optional, he decided.

A note of steel came into his voice. "We're going in," he said, and shoved the stick into a rolling dive. A ghastly weight forced Feinstein back into his seat. Outside the canopy the green earth suddenly leaped and began a massive roll over the airplane.

"There they are! Engaging! I'm engaging!" screamed Egglesby, gripped by the joy of combat. The smile of resignation and death played grimly at the corners of his mouth. The plane stood on its nose and went straight down.

At that moment, Feinstein's stomach revolted. He leaned forward to vomit in his airsick bag just as Major Egglesby entered a turning dogfight with—yes, Major Egglesby could never mistake that flying style—Togo Fuji himself, his plane an agile Zero. In a sustained five-g turn, Feinstein's head suddenly weighted 75 pounds. He found he couldn't lift it. His face stuck between his knees by a terrible force he vomited profusely and miserably into the bag. He wanted to die. He suspected he might. He could barely breathe and his brains were trying to migrate into his spinal cord.

"Ooooagh!" grunted Major Egglesby to relieve the strain. Togo Fuji's plane slid sideways and turned yet tighter, seeking to throw off Major Egglesby's inexorable attack. Like an eagle falling on its prey the major plummeted, turning ever harder, seeking the limits of existence and the airframe. His eyes glittered warmly and a savage satisfaction, which he had first encountered in Captain Marvel comics, flowed hotly into his soul as he realized that he was slowly but surely creeping up and inside on the Zero.

"Ah so, you monster! Chop up children, will you? Little ones? Innocent? Now comes the price!" he exulted, finger tightening on the trigger.

"*Urrrrrghak!*" shrieked Feinstein, who decided he would never eat chipped beef on toast if he thought he would have to look at it again.

"Your moment has come!" Major Egglesby was yelling as the sighting pipper slid slowly onto the cockpit of Togo Fuji's Zero. He was so close that he could see the sallow face of the evil colonel turn to gaze at him, knowing the game was up. For a moment they stared at each other, remembering their many battles over the Tsing Tsong River, the camaraderie of each in his respective camp, the whizzing sword and diced orphans. The dark colonel's face twisted into an unexpected expression. It was ...yes...a smile of death and resignation.

Major Egglesby fired, almost hating to kill a worthy opponent. The heavy thumping of the twenty millimeter sang its vicious song of doom. Fragments of cockpit tore from the Zero as Togo Fuji committed hara-kiri with his last breath.

"Well, how do you like the sport of kings? Eh? Beats being a mere stockbroker, doesn't it? I'll bet you're thinking of going to flight school, eh?" Said Egglesby.

Feinstein pulled his face from his lap and moaned. That night he was able to tell Murphy that the invisible airplanes must exist. He had been in a dog fight with one, he would say, and he hadn't seen a thing.

WITH LYNDON BRAINS

President Lyndon Brains Johnson was on his hands and knees in the Oval Office, his face low over a topographical map of I Corps. Behind him respectfully stood General Ponder, Chairman of the JCS, and a major from protocol in the Pentagon. The President's jowls hung down like wattles and his rump poked up in the manner of an amorous tabby cat. In his hand was a large magnifying glass. He was selecting targets for Colonel Dravidian to bomb in connection with operation Urgent Thumper.

"What's this? Looks like an important road junction, except ... Lookit here! Gawdam roads run in circles! Look! The damn gooks built six circle roads inside each other. We better bomb'em."

The major with General Ponder looked over the copious First Hindquarters and said, "Uh, Mr. President, sir, those aren't roads. They're elevation lines. That's a hill."

The voice from the rug assumed a dangerous growl. The huge face with sagging eye pouches turned on the major like a basset hound.

"Boy, you tryin' to tell me what a road is? I was readin' maps before your daddy gave up sheep, and I know roads when I see roads. You understand, boy?"

"Yessir," said the major, resolving to get out of the Army and go to law school at the first opportunity.

"What you think, Ginral?"

"Roads, Mr. President. Major, if the President of the United States says those elevation lines are roads, then they're roads."

"Yessir."

"Ginral, why you think those rice maggots got roads in circles, inside each other?"

General Ponder wasn't sure how to answer. "Maybe they're fortifying that hill. You know, maybe they figure they can drive trucks real fast to the other side if we attack. They'll always be on the other side, so we can never shoot them."

Lyndon Brains Johnson squinted at the map a moment further. "How those high-yeller peckerheads gonna git trucks onto those roads? They're just circles. They don't connect to anything."

"Airlift, sir," said the major, who was feeling like being a wiseass now that he had decided to go to law school.

"You pullen mah chain, boy?" roared Lyndon Brains Johnson. "Think Ah don't know them little coons got no airplanes? How'd you like to git shot?"

"Mr. President, I was thinking about the invisible airplanes, sir."

The President thought a moment. Maybe the major had something. The President hadn't been able to get a straight answer out of the Pentagon about those damned planes. He gave them every chance, too. It just showed you could lead a horse to drink, but you couldn't make him water. The President suddenly peered more closely through his magnifying glass. His rump rose as his head went down, like a seesaw. Shit! The Central Highlands were just full of those circular roads inside each other! Why the hell hadn't those asskissers in the Pentagon told him? The thing to do was to talk to the right guy direct.

"Get me those intelligence weeners in Danang," he said. "I want to know about those roads."

The White House switchboard activated the satellite link to Danang. Soon the speaker phone on the wall of the Oval Office said, "I'm connecting, sir."

A phone rang far off in Asia and a perky voice said, "Beeboppa Reebop, Rudy T. Toute."

The President's eyes retracted another half inch into their pouches and his jowls sagged. A look of unalloyed hatred spread slowly across his basset-hound features.

"What are you, some kind of fucken rock star?" he roared. "Ginral, I want that goddam peckerhead drowned!"

WASHINGTON WORRIES

In Washington, concern about the menace of the invisible airplanes arched toward a crescendo. The Pentagon expressed grave concern over the erosion of the American edge in technology. Various scientists pointed out that the American edge had been eroding precipitously for three decades, during which the United States had maintained an unchanging lead of fifteen years in all important technologies. Conservatives responded that these hot-house pinkos didn't understand the threat. Congressmen in whose district Invisible Airplane money was to be spent found in their heart a hitherto undiscovered solicitude for the welfare of Our Boys. The people at General Dynamics being no fools, money was slated for every district in the United States.

In various states around the nation, factories began to rise for the production of IADs, or Invisible Airplane Detectors. The design had not yet been finalized, and prototypes suffered from certain growing pains, as for example what seemed an utter inability to detect invisible airplanes. The difficulty was that General Dynamics was unable to say whether there were any invisible airplanes around to be detected, and so wasn't sure whether its device worked. The crux of the problem was that General Dynamics, having no invisible airplanes to experiment with, couldn't tell whether its equipment could in fact detect them. Thus an expensive crash project was begun to design invisible drones. At any rate, when the IAD had finally been thoroughly invented, the factories would stand ready.

Before long, thousands of workers and researchers were drawing paychecks from the program. In the normal course of democratic politics, these people, and the merchants in nearby towns who prospered by selling them clothes and televisions, came to form a powerful constituency for continuing the IAD program. It is usual in democracies that, when enough people earn a livelihood from solving a problem, the problem itself becomes trivial in comparison with the need to keep the solvers employed, so that it becomes crucial not to solve the problem, which has by now become a national resource.

Tensions grew in the vast and growing IAD community, which Marxists, had they adequately understood economics, would have called the contradictions of capitalism. The researchers wanted to avoid inventing a workable detector, so that they could continue their research. The labor unions however wanted to begin production immediately of a detector whether it worked or not. A compromise was reached. The factories would produce an Interim IAD, which wouldn't work, but could be fielded quickly to meet the immediate needs of the Pentagon. The researchers would pursue a Follow-On IAD, or FOIAD, which of course would depend on successful development of invisible drones.

Feinstein said to Corporal Hearn as they bounced and cut through the heavy military traffic in Cowpatch, "Anything new on the invisible airplane front?" He regarded those airplanes as his story, which in fact they seemed to be, inasmuch as the chief source of information was Corporal Hearn. For the same reason Corporal Hearn regarded them as his story.

"No. For three days I've been TDY at BEEB, mailing out medals."

"Medals?"

Hearn swerved to dodge a motor scooter that was trying to ram them and collect damages. Accelerating neatly, he cut around a six-by full of helmets, skirted a noodle stand, and shot into open country.

Three days earlier Corporal Hearn had spent all day in the air-conditioned computer room of BEEB, stuffing Bronze Stars into envelopes addressed by the computer to every lieutenant in Southeast Asia. The military was trying to improve efficiency. Previously medals had been given only to men who had done something courageous in battle, but this had taken a great deal of work, examination of claims, and evaluation of evidence. Besides, those who didn't get medals thought that their career prospects were hurt. Further, many held that winning a medal in combat was a sign of deficient judgment, as anyone who would leap into a trench full of VC and beat them to death with an entrenching tool clearly had a serious personality disorder.

Since there were more men who didn't earn medals than there were who did, numbers made themselves felt and the award of medals had been democratized. The solution had been to award medals by rank, so that every lieutenant got a Bronze Star. For a while the medals were issued on graduation from Officer Candidate School, but it was too hard for people to understand how a lieutenant could have been brave in combat when he hadn't left Virginia. So now they issued them by mail from the computer room. Hearn had spent the next day sending Silver Stars to colonels, and Army Commendation Medals to majors.

While taking a break, Corporal Hearn had picked up a print-out showing the accumulated combat time of Air Force officers. He had noticed one, a Lieutenant Trilling, who had sixteen years of continuous combat flying. A few officers from SAC bases in the US had a couple of years each, but no more, which was strange. He had made a mental note that Feinstein might consider such a tip worth a few bottles.

"Yeah," said Hearn, cutting around an amtrac bellowing and emitting acrid smoke, "They have computers that, you know, keep track of flying hours and things. I didn't know we'd been over here so long. One guy in the Philippines has something like sixteen years combat. One's enough for me."

"Sixteen years? Bullshit. The war's only been on for four." Feinstein put his feet up on the windshield and tore open a candy bar.

"Can't help it," said Hearn with the air of one who can't be held responsible for the vexing ways of the world. "Guy named Lieutenant Gopher Trilling. Or maybe it was Hamster. It's on the printout. A whole bunch of guys in the PI have four years, and even some from back in the World."

"Uhuh. I smell a rat. A lieutenant with sixteen years in combat? He'd be at least a light colonel."

Hearn looked at him with that air of galling confidence that he had. "Bottle of bourbon? For the printout?"

Feinstein chewed and said nothing, screwing his face in thought. Hearn was a real rug merchant. The story on the invisible airplanes was running Feinstein about two cases of hooch a month, and it was beginning to devour his bank balance. At first he had put it on his expense account, and gotten a letter from Accounting in New York saying that AP would pay for treatment in a detox center. Now he was buying Hearn's bribe-hooch with his own money.

Still ...hmmm. Guys with heavy combat hours, in the Philippines? Had to be a spook operation, some kind of secret thing with garrottes and freaky electronics. That would be a story. Besides, if this lieutenant really did have sixteen years of combat flying, that meant the United States had been secretly involved well before the Tonkin Gulf incident. The rank of lieutenant was obviously phony. Jesus, that would blow the press open.

"Yeah. Two bottles, to keep your mouth shut."

"Three."

"Go to hell."

HEARN DISCOVERS TRILLING

In Washington, concern about the menace of the invisible airplanes arched toward a crescendo. The Pentagon expressed grave concern over the erosion of the American edge in technology. Various scientists pointed out that the American edge had been eroding precipitously for three decades, during which the United States had maintained an unchanging lead of fifteen years in all important technologies. Conservatives responded that these hot-house pinkos didn't understand the threat. Congressmen in whose district Invisible Airplane money was to be spent found in their hearts a hitherto undiscovered solicitude for the welfare of Our Boys. The people at General Dynamics being no fools, money was slated for every district in the United States.

In various states around the nation, factories began to rise for the production of IADs, or Invisible Airplane Detectors. The design had not yet been finalized, and prototypes suffered from certain growing pains, as for example what seemed an utter inability to detect invisible airplanes. The difficulty was that General Dynamics was unable to say whether there were any invisible airplanes around to be detected, and so wasn't sure whether its device worked. The crux of the problem was that General Dynamics, having no invisible airplanes to experiment with, couldn't tell whether its equipment could in fact detect them. Thus an expensive crash project was begun to design invisible drones. At any rate, when the IAD had finally been thoroughly invented, the factories would stand ready.

Before long, thousands of workers and researchers were drawing paychecks from the program. In the normal course of democratic politics, these people, and the merchants in nearby towns who prospered by selling them clothes and televisions, came to form a powerful constituency for continuing the IAD program. It is usual in democracies that, when enough people earn a livelihood from solving a problem, the problem itself becomes trivial in comparison with the need to keep the solvers employed, so that it becomes crucial not to solve the problem, which has by now become a national resource.

Tensions grew in the vast and growing IAD community, which Marxists, had they adequately understood economics, would have called the contradictions of capitalism. The researchers wanted to avoid inventing a workable detector, so that they could continue their research. The labor unions however wanted to begin production immediately of a detector whether it worked or not. A compromise was reached. The factories would produce an Interim IAD, which wouldn't work, but could be fielded quickly to meet the immediate needs of the Pentagon. The researchers would pursue a Follow-On IAD, or FOIAD, which of course would depend on successful development of invisible drones.

Feinstein said to Corporal Hearn as they bounced and cut through the heavy military traffic in Cowpatch, "Anything new on the invisible airplane front?" He regarded those airplanes as his story, which in fact they seemed to be, inasmuch as the chief source of information was Corporal Hearn. For the same reason Corporal Hearn regarded them as his story.

"No. For three days I've been TDY at BEEB, mailing out medals."

"Medals?"

Hearn swerved to dodge a motor scooter that was trying to ram them and collect damages. Accelerating neatly, he cut around a six-by full of helmets, skirted a noodle stand, and shot into open country.

Three days earlier Corporal Hearn had spent all day in the air-conditioned computer room of BEEB, stuffing Bronze Stars into envelopes addressed by the computer to every lieutenant in Southeast Asia. The military was trying to improve efficiency. Previously medals had been given only to men who had done something courageous in battle, but this had taken a great deal of work, examination of claims, and evaluation of evidence. Besides, those who didn't get medals thought that their career prospects were hurt. Further, many held that winning a medal in combat was a sign of deficient judgment, as anyone who would leap into a trench full of VC and beat them to death with an entrenching tool clearly had a serious personality disorder.

Since there were more men who didn't earn medals than there were who did, numbers made themselves felt and the award of medals had been democratized. The solution had been to award medals by rank, so that every lieutenant got a Bronze Star. For a while the medals were issued on graduation from Officer Candidate School, but it was too hard for people to understand how a lieutenant could have been brave in combat when he hadn't left Virginia. So now they issued them by mail from the computer room. Hearn had spent the next day sending Silver Stars to colonels, and Army Commendation Medals to majors.

While taking a break, Corporal Hearn had picked up a printout showing the accumulated combat time of Air Force officers. He had noticed one, a Lieutenant Trilling, who had sixteen years of continuous combat flying. A few officers from SAC bases in the US had a couple of years each, but no more, which was strange. He had made a mental note that Feinstein might consider such a tip worth a few bottles.

"Yeah," said Hearn, cutting around an amtrac bellowing and emitting acrid smoke, "They have computers that, you know, keep track of flying hours and things. I didn't know we'd been over here so long. One guy in the Philippines has something like sixteen years combat. One's enough for me."

"Sixteen years? Bullshit. The war's only been on for four." Feinstein put his feet up on the windshield and tore open a candy bar.

"Can't help it," said Hearn with the air of one who can't be held responsible for the vexing ways of the world. "Guy named Lieutenant Gopher Trilling. Or maybe it was Hamster. It's on the printout. A whole bunch of guys in the PI have four years, and even some from back in the World."

"Uhuh. I smell a rat. A lieutenant with eight years in combat? He'd be at least a light colonel."

Hearn looked at him with that air of galling confidence that he had. "Bottle of bourbon? For the printout?"

Feinstein chewed and said nothing, screwing his face in thought. Hearn was a real rug merchant. The story on the invisible airplanes was running Feinstein about two cases of hooch a month, and it was beginning to devour his bank balance. At first he had put it on his expense account, and gotten a letter from Accounting in New York saying that AP would pay for treatment in a detox center. Now he was buying Hearn's bribe-hooch with his own money.

Still...hmmm. Guys with heavy combat hours, in the Philippines? Had to be a spook operation, some kind of secret thing with garrottes and freaky electronics. That would be a story. Besides, if this lieutenant really did have sixteen years of combat flying, that meant the United States had been secretly involved well before the Tonkin Gulf incident. The rank of lieutenant was obviously phony. Jesus, that would blow the press open.

"Yeah. Two bottles, to keep your mouth shut."

"Three."

"Go to hell."

"Where you think this is, Paleface?"

"OK, OK. Three. I hope your liver rots."

DEEP THOUGHT IN THE
FIVE-SIDED WIND TUNNEL

On the third floor of the Pentagon, in the Office of Strategic Creativity and Modular Concepts, General Hogarth Toluene pondered a disturbing series of reports from I Corps. In his teeth he clenched a long black cigarette holder, which served him as a sort of oral swagger stick. He chewed it reflectively and squinted. He didn't like to wear his glasses.

General Toluene looked like the driver in the Greyhound ads on television. He had a richly modulated voice, and was known throughout the Pentagon as a hell of a briefer, a man who could bring tears with nothing but a simple pointer and a flip chart. For these reasons he had risen far and fast in the strategic-thinking community. Insiders in the Pentagon argued that if only he had had a better profile, he would have been the greatest strategist since Clausewitz.

Three reports seemed especially ominous to General Toluene. The first showed the variation over time in the concentration of enemy troops around Danang. A year before, VC battalions had been scattered. Then, suddenly, they had moved closer to the city, and were now gradually, almost imperceptibly tightening the ring. Such things didn't happen without a reason, thought General Toluene. Charlie was up to something.

He frowned. There were odd inconsistencies. Why in August had the enemy battalions suddenly withdrawn several miles and moved generally to the north? What malign chess game were the communists playing? What fiendish end were they working toward?

Perhaps the most unsettling thing, he reflected, was the obvious, sharp increase in the quality of the communist army. A man less versed in strategic thinking and modular concepts would not have noticed, but General Toluene did. In the first place, the shifting of the battalions northward had been done virtually overnight, implying a degree of discipline and organization that General Toluene would have thought impossible. In the second place, the Viet Cong displayed a most worrisome ability to remain hidden in a region thick with American forces. There had been no reports of contact. It was as if all those battalions weren't there. He did not know that in August Colonel Rudyard Thackeray Toute had twisted his elbow while lifting a typewriter, and thus dislocated the entire war.

The second report concerned repeated heavy attacks on the compound of the Third Amphibious Tractor Battalion, just to the north of Danang. General Toluene frowned more deeply and began to drum his manicured fingers on his desk. Why was that particular position so important to the Cong? The other battalions were within easy striking range of the city, yet only an obscure amtrac outfit was hit. Why did Charlie persist in throwing his men against their massed firepower?

He took a drag on his cigarette, slowly elevating the end of the cigarette holder to a rakish upward angle. Once during an important meeting he had been too jaunty in this maneuver. Without his being aware of it, the cigarette had flipped onto the top of his hat, where it had continued burning. He had sat through crucial testimony with a stern expression and smoke pouring from the top of his head, a most embarrassing business. Now he was careful.

The third report had TOP SECRET written on it in red letters.

It was an analysis of the strange matter of the invisible airplanes. In it a pair of engineers from General Dynamics asserted that they had personally seen an American aircraft dogfighting with one of these inexplicable machines. The engineers had offered no explanation but said that more investigation was justified. The tone was somewhat noncommittal. Still, these were high-level design engineers. The communists must have something, from the Russians no doubt—

some advanced device, but...what? Then there was a well-attested
report, signed by General Grommett in fact, of the strafing of an
officers' club in downtown Danang. Several other reports were there
from other positons near the city which had been strafed.

General Toluene rose and began walking slowly in circles
around his desk, cigarette holder elevated like a howitzer. What
was behind the invisible airplanes? All hell was breaking loose over
them. They had been the subject of great attention in Washington's
papers, with right-wing politicians decrying the invisible-airplane
gap and demanding massive investment to catch up. The marketing
department of General Dynamics, claiming that the company had all
the available expertise, was clamoring for a hundred-million-dollar
research contract. Congressional hearings were going to be held
before long.

General Toluene walked thoughtfully to the big wall map of
Vietnam. With little red pins he marked the location of each strafing.
Yes, there was a pattern. The attacks clustered sharply to the north,
just in the region the Viet Cong battalions had occupied following
their sudden relocation.

Suddenly he understood. The northward shift had been practice
for an all-out assault through Happy Valley, and on...yes. His eyes
widened.

General Toluene strode confidently to the telephone and called
the Chief of Staff, General Walter Ponder.

"Sir, this is Hog Toluene. I'm sorry to bother you, but I have
something I think you ought to see. If my reports here are right it
looks as though the communists are getting ready to...." His voice
dropped to a whisper dripping with condensed significance. "Capture
Danang"

General Ponder was an artilleryman and didn't hear well.
"What?"

"Yessir."

"Yessir, what?" said General Ponder with irritation.

"Yessir, sir."

"Goddamit, yessir, sir, what?"

"Sir, yessir, sir, sir. Sir."

"Any more of this bird-brained crap and you get a court martial. What the hell is wrong?"

The conversation wasn't going as General Toluene had hoped. "The commies are going to capture Danang."

"Horse shit."

"I hope so, sir. But I'd hate to be wrong and the evidence looks, well, solid."

General Ponder thought for a moment. The idea sounded lunatic. On the other hand, if Danang somehow did fall, the Chairman of the Joint Chiefs would probably be blamed, and that would be the end of his career. And who the hell knew what was going on over there? His intelligence people sure didn't. Maybe the smart thing would be to bring someone else into it.

"Bring that stuff up here. I'll let Wurther know."

In the Jungle. Saving Democracy

Second Platoon Bravo Company humped through the agonizing heat toward the An Dong River in dead silence. The sun beat down like a soft rubber truncheon and the humidity hung at an asphyxiating hundred percent. Even the condoms on their rifle barrels were limp and dispirited. Second Platoon was noted for its aggressiveness in not finding the enemy. At this moment they were making a supreme effort not to find him, reaching down into their souls for that final ounce of failure that made the difference between death and beer.

Lieutenant William Washington, the only black platoon commander in I Corps, said "OK, chillun, this playground is now in recess." They dropped heavily to the ground near a shattered temple and reached for canteens.

"Think the bastard's going to get us, Lieutenant?" asked Ron Cagle, a dark-haired corporal from Tennessee.

"Huh. Charles ain't smart enough to kill this nigger. I'm going to bring all my men home from this war, every swinging dick, and just incidentally me too. In fact, maybe just a bit more than incidentally. Don't you trust me and my leadership qualities?"

"Yessir. But Charlie's a lot worse than the rest. He's gonna kill us, I tell you."

"Oh, he's trying. He's trying, all right. But he ain't going to do it."

Charlie was their battalion commander, Colonel Charles Aa es Kelley. He was indeed trying to kill Second Platoon. So, though t a lesser extent, were the Viet Cong. Colonel Kelley needed casualties to show that he was a hard-charging, pugnacious officer who took t ie battle to the enemy and gave him no rest. In a more reasonable wa if there were such, he could have done this by having his men captur a city. In Vietnam there was nothing to capture that.was worth havi g, so the best measure of effectiveness was the number of casualt es his men took. Moreover there was an unofficial contest between ie Army and Marines to produce the most casualties, thus continuin a rivalry reaching back to Tarawa.

Colonel Kelley consequently had his men patrolling constan ly where he thought the thickest concentrations of enemy might e found. Fortunately his information came from REBOP, where as low-level tactical intelligence it was compiled alphabetically b a lieutenant. On the first of the month he reported concentrations of enemy troops in all villages beginning with A, one the second in those beginning with B, and so on. Since this intelligence was alm st always wrong, many lives were saved.

Cagle leaned his head on his helmet, lit a cigarette, and bl w a cloud of smoke over his head. "Ain't this great? Seeing all th se foreign places? You guys know you love it."

"Fuck you, Prevert. You wouldn't even be here if you wasn a child molester...Hey, Newbie, you know why old Prevert's a Muhre 1? Tell'im, Prevert."

Cagle thought a moment. He had told the tale dozens of tim s. He was used to it.

"Shit, it wasn't nothing," he said. "I was working in Kriegste t's Esso back home, see, and this lady pulls in driving a Corvair. Well, s ie sorta mumbles something, which was, 'Do you have a rest room ' I couldn't hear too good, and I thought she said, 'Do you have a wh k broom?' So I says, 'Naw, lady, but I can blow it out for you with e air hose.'

"Well, it turns out she's the mayor's wife and she starts shriek n' and tears outa there like she had a burr up her ass and pretty so n ol' Sherriff Powell comes out in the squad car and tells me I'm un er arrest for Salacious Degradation or some shit, and Judge Wilson t lls me I can do two in the Corps or four in the slammer, and I chose wrong."

"Sounds about right. I was...."

The sound of chopper blades came in the distance. The sound grew until a Huey dropped to the ground. Mike Feinstein jumped out like a hairy underfed insect and walked, crouching, toward Second Platoon through low vegetation blowing in the rotor wash. The chopper fwop-fwopped faster and rose, roaring and whining, into the clear blue sky.

"Afternoon. You Lieutenant Washington?" asked Feinstein.

"I have that distinction. Can't help it. Am I being relieved of my command, I dearly hope?"

Lieutenant Washington had never seen anybody sweat like this white guy. If you squeezed a sodden sponge, he thought, less water would pour out. Where did it come from? This scrawny muthufucker musta weighted three hunnerd pounds this morning and now he's down to it looks like about ninety.

"Not by me. I'm just a commie minion of the press. UPI." He held out a press card.

"Oh. Well, you should report that I ought to be relieved. My men, too. And sent home in disgrace. Or any other way."

Feinstein had never encountered an officer who made sense before. He found it disturbing. He wasn't sure how to begin.

"Maybe this is going to sound crazy, but, well, there's this report going around about how the Russians have these invisible airplanes." He suddenly realized he sounded like a raving lunatic. "Supposedly they fly over this sector. Fuck, I feel stupid. Still, I gotta ask. You guys seen anything like that?"

Lieutenant Washington was about to ask the obvious, namely how the hell do you see something that's invisible, when Cagle said,

"Lieutenant, you reckon that head case in the F-4...I mean he always looks like he's trying to fight somebody, but ain't nobody there."

Lieutenant Washington thought hard for a moment. Damn, maybe...yeah, that Phantom did look like he was chasing something, and he was always shooting at what looked like nothing. Shit, maybe them Russians....

An hour later Feinstein waited for his chopper to return. He wanted a drink. He had firm reports, from a dozen apparently sane Marines, confirming the existence of the invisible intruders. What the hell was going on?

VOGLE

Corporal Hearn dropped Zeke Feinstein off at the Piao-Lyang-de Pigu Hotel and blended into the chaotic traffic to pick up Paul Vogle, the chief of the Danang Bureau of UPI. Headquarters had assigned him to drive Vogle around for a day. It was a way of keeping reporters under a degree of control. Hearn had never met Vogle, but thought he might make a useful addition to his efforts in the line of invisible airplanes. He stopped at 19 Ngo De Ke Street and found a small colonial villa set amid palm trees. At his knock an old, low voice said, "Come in." He did, and found himself, dear god, in dim air-conditioned coolness. At first he could see little in the dimness.

"Mr. Vogle?"

"Have a drink."

His eyes adjusted. A thin late-fortyish man, hair thinning badly, sat at a table with a half-empty bottle of bambdebam in front of him. His face was narrow, sallow, and almost emaciated. Or maybe the eyes just made him look emaciated. He looked drunk and tired, very tired, maybe incurably tired.

"Sir, I'm not supposed to drink on duty."

"I know you're not. Have a drink, for god's sake."

"Yessir. Thank you sir."

"Don't call me sir. You sound like you're in the Marines or something." There was an edge to his voice, an impatience, as of one who just didn't want to hear any more of it. Of anything.

"Yessir. I mean, yes."

The thin figure pushed the bottle across the table. A cigarette

97

leaned from the other hand, the fingers stained yellow by nicoti e. An ashtray, in the shape of an elephant's head with the top of he cranium removed, was almost full of stubs. He didn't look healt y, though Hearn. Nothing specific. He just looked…used up.

"Here, pour it yourself, kid. Sit down. Don't worry. If you're l e, blame it on me." He pushed a glass at Hearn, who sat. He pou d himself a small drink and took a sip. It tasted like brake fl id mixed with cough syrup. He had never had Vietnamese liqu r. The troops were not allowed to associate with the Vietnamese. T e command feared that they might develop unwholesome sympathi s. Consequently Hearn drank only Feinstein's classy hooch.

When Vogle said nothing, Hearn finally said, "Uh, where ar I supposed to take you, sir?"

Nothing. Vogle, who by his looks might have been a disillusion d desert father, stared at the table. After a moment, he said, "I freaki g forget. No, I'm lying. I'm supposed to go look at the remains of so e of your friends roasted in an amtrac." He stopped. Then, "You thi k I want to?" .

"I don't know sir."

"They never learn, do they?"

"Who, sir?"

"The Marines."

Silence.

"Why do you think the Marines have amtracs here?"

"Uh, to fight the gooks, sir."

Vogle said nothing again. He took a large gulp of bamdeba n. Hearn's eyes widened. This guy could pack it down. One day th y might put him in a jar in a museum.

"No. No, they have amtracs here because they have amtracs. It wasn't exactly anger that gave the voice its abrasive edge, more l ke the burnt-out ashes of an anger that had gnawed itself to death. "Do amtracs make any goddam sense here? Gasoline tank in the botto n, roof to bounce against, biggest target in Vietnam? No, they ha ve amtracs here because they're in the table of organization, and thi is the only war they've got, so they're going to use the amtracs."

"Is that really why, sir?"

Vogle looked even more tired, which was an accomplishment. "How old are you?"

"Twenty-one, sir."

"How long have you been here?"

"Three months, sir."

Vogle covered his face with his palms. "Twenty-three years for me."

After a minute he said, "I'll probably get thrown out of country for subverting you. Listen, kid. The military does what it knows how to do, not what it needs to do. A military man only knows how to do one thing, and he does it in response to everything. Ask a tank officer if he knows how to bake a cake. 'Sure I do,' he says. 'First you adjust the track tension....' He can't adapt. He doesn't know what the word means. Do you think it makes sense to have supersonic fighters doing close-air support? They can't even see the ground at that speed. Oh, hell. Let's go."

Hearn sensed that he was in the presence of something new, something that hadn't occurred to him. This wasn't the ooorah pep-and-good-news talk of the officers. It wasn't the cynical armor of the guys he worked with. It was something old and worn and terribly... "used up" was the phrase that came again to mind.

"Yessir." Hearn stood up.

"No, siddown. Hell with it. Have another drink."

Hearn did. He was about to learn about the war. He didn't know what he would tell his boss. He would think of something.

AIR DEFENSE CHECKS IN

At ten o'clock in the clinging hot darkness of Danang, trucks and jeeps began to pull up to the radar bunker of the air field. The Big One was coming. Nervous drivers stopped too quickly, eliciting curses from the tense men riding in the back. To the north gunships poured red death at the earth as Third Tracs beat off another furious attack, the night shuddering with artillery and the tearing sound of miniguns. The radar technicians scrambling from the trucks paid no attention.

"Hustle up," growled Sgt. Manuel Pedro Gonzales de Sebastian de la Madrid de la Hijo del Gusanito de Cordoba, who ran the big search radars that could detect at a range of 200 miles the bombers that the North Vietnamese didn't have.

The doors of the radar room opened and the men poured in, racing to the consoles with the big green screens. Tension filled the air like a fluid.

"Come on! Come on!" urged the sergeant.

"Hey, cut us some slack, sarge," muttered the corporal who worked the altitude-finding radar.

Sgt. Manuel Pedro Gonzales de Sebastian de la Madrid de la Hijo del Gusanito de Cordoba tried. He tried hard at everything because, although he was only a sergeant, he was aware of having sprung from a family of great historical importance. In the fifteenth century, the great church of Cordoba, then a small mudwalled town, had contained the greatest collection of relics in all Spain. There were six pieces of wood from the True Cross, all of different kinds of wood, which was held to show the miraculous powers of the godhead.

There were two pounds of nails from the True Cross, a molar from Saint Peter, a cup made of Spanish clay and used at the last supper, and three sandals from Luke himself.

There was some degree of controversy over the sandals. One school of thought held that St. Luke had two pairs of shoes, and one sandal had been lost. Another thought the three sandals showed that St. Luke miraculously had three legs, and that anyone who doubted this lacked faith. A religious war had ensued over this matter in which fifteen thousand people were killed.

The most important relic however was the Holy Doorknob from the inn that turned away Joseph and Mary. No other church in all Christendom had such a thing, perhaps because no one else had thought of it. One night it disappeared. The distraught priests began a frantic search of the neighborhood. A small boy suddenly pointed to a thicket and shouted, *"Por alla! El Gusanito nos lo muestra!"* Sure enough, below a caterpillar hanging from a twig, the doorknob was found.

This was held to be a sign that the small boy's line was blessed by God, and he, in his manhood, was made a count and given the honorific title "Hijo del Gusanito de Cordoba." He became a respected minor noble, and never stole another doorknob.

Lt. David Miller, in command of the night shift, watched and tried to conceal his worry. Normally he loved radar. In fact, he thought that probably the world would be a better place if it consisted only of green blips silently moving on circular glass screens.

He was, in fact, a consummate radar chauvinist. At night, walking to his hooch in the officers' compound, he often thought sneeringly of human vision, operating as it did on excessively short wavelengths. He loved to think of his long vertically polarized beams, reaching far out, overcoming the forth-power law, and detecting distant objects.

Tonight he was, if not frightened, at least anxious. Like many soldiers with no experience of war, he wondered how he would behave when the crunch came. It wasn't fair, he thought briefly, that in his first month he should be in charge of the world's busiest airport with all hell about to break loose. He felt he ought to do something to show Leadership. He wasn't sure what.

"Men," he said, "I want you to stay by your posts no matter what happens. War is war, and I want the 354th Radar Support Services Group to be remembered with honor." He thought a moment. "That's the most goddam preposterous thing I've ever said."

"Yessir," said Sgt. Will Ferguson, tuning the auxiliary transmitter with hurrying fingers. "Don't let it bother you, sir. All the officers say things like that. It's to keep our morale up."

"Does it?" asked Lt. Miller, suddenly curious. "I mean, keep your morale up?"

"Don't need to, sir. I just stay high on nature."

The big green finger of the search strobe began to sweep in rhythmic circles. The sergeant began his check list. "Main trans? OK. Aux One? OK. Aux Two? Hurry up, Peterson, we got twenty minutes before they hit us. Then we're up to our ass in alligators. Autopilot? OK. Directors? Get those fuckers on-line, Jones. Do it."

The equipment running, the 354th Radar-Support Services Group leaned tensely over their screens, waiting. They were good, but from what they had been able to learn, the night would be bad, and each wondered how he would handle it.

"Oh, shit. Contact bearing 324, range 21.2. Oh, motherfucker, here they come."

"Plot?"

"Got it, Sir."

"Contact, bearing 232, range 180. Contact bearing 122, range 194. Contact...." The screens were filling.

It happened every month. He didn't know why. Many hundreds of blips, all belonging to the US military, mysteriously converged on Viet Nam. And he had to track all those aircraft and then fill out paperwork. It was hell.

Far out over the South China Sea, a KC-135 tanker from Guam roared through the night en route to U Ta Pao in Thailand, unaware of the growing panic at Danang. Far below the light of the moon reflected in silver splendor from the rumpled cloud cover. In the austere passenger bay above the huge fuel bladders, General Richard "Beefeater" Thompson, commander of Andersen Field at Guam, took a swig from a bottle of bourbon, wiped his mouth, and said to several full colonels, adequately lubricated, who listened attentively,

"Shit, with this juice going for fifty cents a quart, a man can't afford to stay sober. Cheaper'n milk."

The colonels laughed appreciatively. In an obscure seat Lieutenant Trilling smiled enough to show appreciation but not enough to call attention to himself. He had been making these flights for years now, and knew better than to enter uninvited into a field-grade conversation. His watery eyes gleamed with pleasure. He was thinking of the bundle he had made when the stock of General Dynamics had gone up twelve points on the news that it had gotten a major contract for invisible-airplane detectors. He really needed the tax break he got by flying with General Thompson.

Early in the war, Congress had come under pressure from the Pentagon to ease the financial burden on the common soldier who fought for his country in Asia. A lurid picture was painted of corporal's wives leaving babies alone in rickety fire-trap housing that enlisted men lived in while they went to night jobs in sweat shops. Consequently a bill had been passed allowing a $1000 tax deduction for every month a man spent in combat, the thought being to compensate for income lost to a man's family by keeping him from moonlighting.

As the bill advanced through committee, a certain amount of sculpting had taken place. A thousand dollars seemed excessive for enlisted men, so their credit was cut to $500. Since "combat" wasn't easy to define in a murky war, being in the combat zone at any place was accepted as being in combat. Exactly what was meant by "month spent in combat" wasn't clear, so the committee, at the Pentagon's suggestion, had decided that any part of a month counted as a month. "Month" was interpreted to mean "calendar month." Finally, "combat zone" was interpreted to include the air space above Vietnam, and the contiguous air space to a distance of 100 nautical miles.

Someone had then noticed that a man could get two months tax credit by flying over Vietnam at midnight on the last day of the month. This didn't make sense, but the bored technician who wrote the accounting program had slipped up. Suddenly literally hundreds of planes began flying from every base in Asia on the 31st, grasping at any expedient that might bring them in contact with precious Vietnamese air space. Freighters in droves swept in from Japan, to land at Bangkok and refuel. The tankers discovered that, by flyi 1g empty, they could reach U Ta Pao from Guam. B-52s from Oklaho 1a swooped over, trailed by tankers. All training missions went e: t. Aircraft carriers nudged the coast so pilots could dash by.

The first time this occurred, the radar watch officer in the No th Vietnamese capital had taken one look at his screens and collaps :d of a heart attack. Three hundred thirty-seven planes arriving w th perfect precision: He had known it wasn't smart to provoke 1e Americans. Every MiG in North Viet Nam had scrambled.

A MATTER OF LANGUAGE

In the darkened conference room at Cornell, a cloud of neat Van Dyke beards waved around the mahogany table like fronds of undersea vegetation, rising to wire-rimmed glasses and then to the wildly unkempt hair of the academically tenured. As General Ponder, Chairman of the Joint Chiefs of Staff, rewound the tape recorder, the brightest lights of America's linguists waited expectantly, men who knew the subtlest nuances of Proto-Urdu, Lower Twandwit, and the rare dialect of Sastabi, spoken only by a tribe of three breech-clouted sheepherders in the Olduvai Gorge. These luminaries had assembled at the urgent request of the Defense Intelligence Agency, all expenses paid, to ponder a dangerous new turn in the war.

General Ponder reached forward and turned a switch. A thin hiss filled the room as the tape began, then the rustle of branches and the faint twitter of birds.

"Ook," whispered a voice, obviously trying to make as little sound as possible, "Ook-ook. Nani batawa? Tubong san-dalati."

A burst of static followed, then an answering, "Waba dai ookbang, swahnauta noo pah trane ma?" A tone of deep puzzlement was evident in the voice, the high pitch of which suggested that the speaker was from a race of small build.

"Su cahni lalong dookubi trane sondwanoo pahgah si tala tala sehret yun, nani? Fah!"

"Dwei, sehret yun, yuk!"

A deeper, more resonant voice came on the net, emanating from the fuller rib cage of a Caucasian. "Twan ook sehret yun hau. Hau!"

Toute had noticed this, and suggested that the mysterious mercenaries had Russian leaders. The conversation lasted another thirty seconds, then suddenly ceased. Colonel Rudyard Thackeray Toute's Radio Intercept division had picked it up coming from the high forests of the upper Annamese Finger, and found that no one could translate it.

This was not the first transmission in the unknown dialect. A suspicious intercept operator had heard for a week several transmissions in what he thought had been the same language, but managed to record only this one. Colonel Toute had sent the tape through channels back to the Defense Language Institute in Monterrey, California, with an analysis suggesting that the Soviets might be bringing in foreign mercenaries for some sort of surprise operation. He had noted the deeper voice and suggested that the mercenaries might have Russian commanders. Colonel Toute had by this time decided that the most important function of intelligence was to be interesting, and everybody thought mercenaries were interesting.

The Institute had been unable to translate it. The Defense Intelligence Agency had immediately grasped the gravity of the situation, implying as it did a major escalation of the war, and convened the tweeded linguists.

Professor Johan Blenchfedder, head of the linguistics department at Indiana University, put the tips of his fingers together and slowly worked them. "I don't know," he said reflectively, "I just don't know. The lack of sibilants is pronounced, which rules out the inferior Palanganese dialects. I believe I'd recognize even a degenerate inferior Palanganese—but the tonal system just isn't there, so...."

A minor commotion began at the far end of the table. Dr. Claude Polinaire of Cornell began shaking violently, hair flying as if in orbit. His thin face purpled with anguish, or perhaps agony, as the symptoms of epilepsy crept over him. The circumambient van Dykes turned toward him with a rustle of worn tweed and waited for him to speak. Polinaire was young, but known already as the leading authority on the Tahjong grammars of eastern Unna.

"No. Not Micronesian, and not a trace, not a sign, of Sephardoumanian gutturals." His voice rose to a shriek.

Dr. Sven Unlufter broke in, "But...'tala tala'...reduplicative verbs suggest an island construct. If of course "tala" can be taken to be a verb."

"Which it can't," growled Robert Trondheim of Quebec. "And I still think the terminal "mah" is a corrupt Sinitic interrogative marker, with the entire tonal system lost of course."

"No! No! No!" shrieked Polinaire, shaking spasmodically. "How... How do you account for 'tran-du,' I ask you? The only long 'a' in the entire transcript? How?"

General Ponder listened to the quarrel, as he had been doing for three hours, with a sense of having been dropped unexpectedly, and undeservedly, into a room full of Martians. These men all thought different things, he noted disapprovingly. How could they get anything done if they thought different things? And they slouched. Slouching was bad. Further, they had all that hair, and beards to boot. Something about their faces kept tugging at his mind, something about the round puff of tangles with the beard projecting below. Finally it came to him: They looked like a bunch of goddam coonskin hats. This place was right out of Alice and Wonderland, he decided, not stopping to remember where coonskin hats occurred in Alice.

He cleared his throat with a booming noise, which he had noticed seemed to quiet them.

"*Ha-rooom*! Gentlemen, the Defense Department appreciates your assistance, but can't we come to a conclusion?" he said, watching Blenchfedder slowly pumping his finger tips. Looks like spiders fucking, thought General Ponder.

Blenchfedder was silent for a moment as his mind raced over the fascinating dialect of the tape. His fingers pumped faster, disturbing General Ponder. Fricatives bubbled through Blenchfedder's consciousness like pipe smoke, declensions and ablatives and Indo-European particles whirred and whirled and nothing came out. The damned tape just didn't compute. He drifted back to consciousness of the room and saw the broad, green-suited general with rows and rows of red and purple and yellow medals. That man looks like a tossed salad, he thought, and said,

"General, it would appear that we can't come to a conclusion."

General Ponder was puzzled. They were supposed to agree on

something, but he couldn't tell them what to agree on. How did civilians get anything done with nobody to tell them what to agree on?

"Why not? Do you want to hear the tape again?"

"There is no conclusion to come to. We don't know what language it is."

General frowned. "Why don't you know? You're linguists, aren't you? Linguists know about languages."

That's what they were for, he thought. Hmmm. Well, if they didn't know what language it was, they at least knew what language it wasn't.

"Then guess. The Army needs a conclusion. It's not European. It isn't Chinese. It isn't Montagnard. It isn't all sorts of other things. What's left?"

Blenchfedder looked at him with new respect. He was right. They could at least narrow it down.

"Well, gentlemen?"

Trondheim said, "Yes. The trouble is that we have among us scholars who know all of the language groups of the world. That is to say, when you have eliminated all possibilities, nothing is left. Our conclusion then would have to be that the tape doesn't exist."

"Excellent!" said General Ponder, reaching for the recorder. "That sure solves that, doesn't it?" All of these hours to decide the tape didn't exist, something they could have decided in thirty seconds

THE SWINE IN CONCERT

General Grommett sat in the front row with Colonel Drinelly, Colonel Droningkeit, and Colonel Dravidian in a section roped off for field-grade officers. Thousands of Marines were filing into stands hastily built around an elevated stage of beach netting and two-by-fours. Diesel generators thumped in the night to provide electricity for the lights. General Grommett felt hopeful. Things were looking up, and he thought the concert would be a Shot in the Arm for his image. He needed a lift, what with the matter of the invisible airplanes and the repeated attacks on the Third Tracs compound.

In particular this concert would benefit his reputation for concern for the common soldier. Walther had arranged to seat the press where General Grommett could easily be photographed enjoying the music, which would show his easy camaraderie with the troops. He had worried a bit about the Gadarene Swine, who didn't look to embody wholesome American values. He remembered a Newsweek picture of the leader with his face painted like a spider's and clutching what, no matter how the general turned the picture, appeared to be a chicken's head. Colonel Walther had assured him that the Swine were on the approved list. No doubt the Newsweek picture pertained to a costume party.

General Grommett turned and gazed over the assembled Marines with a firm but fair smile. They were men a general could be proud of—clean, neat, and respectful to their superiors. They had these qualities because they were rear-echelon clerks and PX employees. General Grommet had toyed with flying in troops from the field, but decided against it. They were always muddy and frequently didn't obey regulations regarding shaving. While he could understand weakness in the lower orders, he didn't think it appropriate to reward such behavior, and anyway reporters were present.

Something resembling quiet fell. Artillery boomed softly in the distance, indistinct and soothing, and mortar flares trembled on the outer bounds of Marine existence. A Red Cross girl in blue vertical candy stripes announced the performance. There were many unseemly whistles, noted General Grommett disapprovingly. A black accent from Hearn's direction yelled, "Take it off!"

From the stage Klok Mortuary, born Billy Beemis in North Cleveland seventeen years earlier, peered with red-lidded eyes at the audience. He wore filthy jeans, clutched a metal-flake-blue electric guitar, and had shoulder-length hair well on the way to being a minor ecosystem. His consciousness was bleary with cannabis residue and demanding concert schedules. He tried to concentrate. Who were these people, he wondered? Why were they wearing those green clothes? They looked like fascists. He hated them, he decided. The lights began to melt the grease paint that made his face into a ghastly black-and-red spider's mask. It oozed into his eyes and burned. He squinted resentfully.

Gotta quit blowen that boss reefer, he thought. Just for a couple of days, clean out his mind. The old lungs were going, too, and his throat was always sore. Shit. Hey, what the fuck was going on? The acid must be starting to hit. The crowd merged, swam out of focus, blurred into some weird-shit wallpaper with lots of heads. Jeez.

Klok absently scratched his enormous electric-pink codpiece, raising hoots from those dangerous-looking thugs. He tried to direct his attention to them. They seemed to be waiting for him to do something. What could it be? Play, that was it. This must he a gig. He looked around. Yeah, the band was here. That was it. A gig. He gathered together as much of his being as was immediately available to him.

"OK," he said wearily, "Let's jam for these assholes."

Then he attacked the guitar as if trying to dismember it.

Waaaaannnnggg!....waanng! Waaannnng! The skies shuddered, it being a principle of rock that enough amplification substituted for technique. The drummer and sax man kicked in on different beats. The effect was what a reviewer for Time had called "a bold escape from the tyranny of outdated western music theory." In penance, the Time reviewer had then gone to a bar for the evening.

Klok threw his head back and emitted a shrill adolescent whine, "Waaaaaaaaaaangaaawaaaaannnnnnnngzooonnnnnnnkawakaka kawaaaaaaaaaaannnnnnnnnnnnnnnnnnn!"

"Uggawugawuggagawugga capitalist pig! Don't gonna suck on my ree-fer cig!" His voice rose several decibels to a chain-saw screech. "Blood! Blood! Blood of the people!"

General Grommett's eyes narrowed and a green cast came over his cultivated mahogany visage. Something had gone badly wrong. Who had let that anti-American creature up there? His values didn't look wholesome. Was it too late to stop it? A tight feeling came over his midriff. He suspected that this concert wasn't after all going to be a Shot in the Arm. It looked more like a Kick in the Balls.

"My mo-o-ther! Mo-o-o-ther! She's like a capitalist rope! Ta-ken, taa-a-aken, taken 'way mah dope!"

The Gadarene Swine zonked, waaannged and screeched, twitched and jerked and whinnied and rutted. The stage lights changed colors, eerily reflecting on the smoke and haze. The sax man blew squawking atonal riffs and tried, just enough off the beat to be irritating, to copulate with his instrument. Klok Mortuary barked and neighed and ululated over the cataclysmic flow of sound. He pounded alternately on the guitar and his codpiece.

"Mer-ka! Mer-ka! Home of the grave and Satan! Sex crime! Sex crime! Let's do some syncopatin'!"

By the end of the first set, Anesthesia was thoroughly drunk. The concert was the only reasonable thing he had seen in the Corps. The Swine had reinvigorated his lost sense of rightness. He determined to join the performers. He wasn't sure why. Somehow Klok came closer than Colonel Droningkeit to his vision of the true and the good. The Swine wouldn't, he was sure, take away a man's pearl-handled forty-fives.

"Hey, Swine!" He lurched to his feet as Hearn grabbed desperately for his collar. "Hoo! Shee-it! You wide muhfuhs all right! Heah I come! Gack!" Hearn had managed to grab his collar.

"Siddown, you drunken idiot!"

"Leggo, Hearn! I be goan join de Swine, ain't goan be in de w th no mo'!"

He struggled erect again as Larry grabbed his arm. Bea s, committed to a policy of imitation in lieu of comprehension, hu g on to a leg. They swayed momentarily, a weaving eruption in a sea of green.

"...waaangalongawonkawonkawaaang!   Revoluuuu-tic n! Revoluuuu-cion! It's the age of sacrifice! Poultry! Poultry! Who go ta boxa rice?"

"Hot dawg! Chicken be comin' now!" said Anesthesia. He sho k free of Larry and staggered forward, Hearn clinging to his back.

Stage attendants ran onto the clanging brilliance of the stage w th a fifty-gallon aquarium containing the Swine's celebrated colony of pet army ants. The function of these military insects was to eat t e chicken after Klok had wrung from it all of its artistic potential, in addition to its head. The attendants then stood discretely offsta ze with cans of ant spray. Art was art, but there had been insurar ce problems when the things had swarmed off stage in Des Moines.

The swine were working themselves into an epileptic frenzy. Kl k Mortuary played his guitar between his legs like a fretted phall s. Suddenly the reached into his codpiece and pulled out...

Good god, gasped General Grommett to himself, nearing t e point of explosion. It looked like a chicken. It was a chicken. Ie remembered the picture in Newsweek. The horrible truth dawn d on him. This disaster had to stop, now. That hairy little draft-evac er seemed to be strangling the animal. Something had to be do e. General Grommett doubted seriously whether any general had e er made chief of staff after sponsoring a teen-age degenerate in a d y-glo codpiece who fed chickens to army ants.

He leaped up. "Stop this!" he roared. "The concert is over! D s-missed!"

Nobody heard him.

Frantically he turned to the audience with his arms in the ir, bellowing for attention. Several thousand pairs of eyes remair d focused on Klok, who had produced a butcher knife from t e utilitarian depths of the codpiece. Apparently he was about to cle n the chicken.

"Atten-hut!" bellowed General Grommett.

Nothing happened. He noticed a large black soldier struggling through the mass of onlookers, another Marine riding on his back. What was going on? He had to stop this.

General Grommett climbed onto the stage in a blind fury just behind Anesthesia and the attached Hearn, and headed for Klok, who had the knife raised over the limp mass of feathers. Anesthesia was yelling something incomprehensible about wanten his fuggin nuke-you-ler bummer. The saxophone squonked and wawked. Behind General Grommett came Colonel Droningkeit and behind him, Larry and Beans, all aiming to rescue their respective principals.

Klok looked up, saw the small mob rushing at him, and dropped the knife in terror. They were after him. Doubtless they wanted to despoil him. He had suspected it all along. Maybe he had better lay off acid for a while. He leaped to his feet and prepared to retreat. They could have his chicken, he thought, but not his guitar. He fled to one end of the stage, but couldn't escape. The odd green men were everywhere. He turned to face his persecutors. That funny-looking one with those weird stars on his collar seemed murderous.

"Not my guitar! Pigs!"

He scurried away from them, thrusting the guitar high in the air as if to hold it beyond their reach. General Grommett caught him and began reaching over his head for the guitar. He didn't want the guitar, but on the other hand he wasn't sure what he did want, and the guitar seemed to be the only thing available. Colonel Droningkeit did likewise because General Grommett was doing it. Larry and Beans appended themselves to the pile and clutched at Anesthesia. For a moment they stood in frozen struggling tableau while flashbulbs exploded and the audience cheered mightily.

The pose, appearing on the covers of dozens of magazines in the ensuing weeks was psychedelic Iwo Jima, with Klok Mortuary and his guitar as flagpole, except for the pink codpiece billowing out before like a low-flying dirigible. A Marine general inexplicably seemed to be trying to help hold the guitar aloft. And why was the corporal riding a black man like a horse? Many asked this and other questions. General Grommett's prospects of becoming chief of staff declined precipitately.

THE END

Paul Vogle awoke in the dim chill of his living room with a throbbing hangover. It was how he usually awoke. He was used to it. His mouth tasted like the inside of a truck driver's glove. He was used to that, too. Lizards fucked urk-urk-urk on the wall and a fly buzzed lazily in the background.

He groped for a cigarette. Then he poured a stiff bamdebam on the hair-of-dog principle. Maybe it would help. He felt like shit. He wondered whether he could stand up, and then wondered why he might want to. He did not believe that anything he did materially affected anything at all. UPI paid for the bamdebam, though. Somehow he would stand up.

Damn, he thought, ashen memory creeping back into his aching head like an unwanted relative. New York wanted a feature on Our Wounded Boys. Yeah, that was it. Oh, God, how splendid. He would catch a cyclo to the Naval Support Activity Hospital through the luminous green countryside that he so loved, that was his agonized home now, with its people who had somehow become part of him and who had no idea why their families got caught in napalm attacks and charred crisp, and he would walk down the wards of the blinded, the faceless, the burn cases from exploded amtracs, under sheets of plastic covered with moisture from evaporating serum, the gut-shot kids awaiting a lifetime relationship with a colostomy bag, kids who didn't know where Viet Nam was or why they were there, and he would squirt off some bullshit or other into the teletype for the five o'clock lead.

Another day in Viet Nam. He poured himself more bamdebam. A water glass, full.